215099

Clinical Death

Patricia A. Bremmer

Elusive Clue Series

Put a little mystery in your life!

Patricia A. Bremmer

Clinical Death

Copyright © 2008

by

Patricia A. Bremmer

ISBN 978-0-9745884-6-9

Cover Design by Martin Bremmer

For additional copies contact:

**Windcall Publishing/
Windcall Enterprises**
75345 RD. 317
Venango, Ne 69168

www.windcallenterprises.com

www.patriciabremmer.com

12-08-14

Acknowledgements

My thanks and acknowledgements to all who helped create **"Clinical Death"**.

Martin Bremmer, my husband, who took over my daily tasks so I could steal away to a private place to write.

Jamie Swayzee, for the hours and hours of grueling work on editing.

Detective Glen Karst, who used his expertise in his field to keep my crime scenes believable, while allowing me to abuse his persona in my book.

Jack Sommars, my friend and screenplay writer, for his final editorial review.

Eloise Hughes, for proofreading the first draft.

Animal Clinic of Ogallala, Nebraska, for allowing us to photograph their caduceus for the front cover.

Cover Design by **Martin Bremmer.** Martin can take any design from my mind and produce it perfectly on the computer. Thanks Honey!

Chapter 1

Becky Harrington looked up from the pile of work on her desk when she heard the door chime indicating another client on this busy Monday morning. Her eyes rested on the figure of a man dressed in tight blue jeans and a black western hat. His muscular frame could not hide behind the loose fitting button-down shirt. She instantly noticed his arm in a sling—probably a rodeo accident. She envisioned him mounting an angry snorting bull, hurling snot, eagerly waiting for the gate to open to rid himself of the uninvited rider.

Dr. Calvin J. Getsbowm walked in, disrupting her dreamlike vision of the handsome cowboy.

"Glen, what the hell brings you here? And what the hell did you do to your arm?"

Becky rearranged her long braids, pretending to be too busy with her paperwork to notice the conversation between the men.

Glen, a slight blush infusing his tanned face, hated attention being drawn to him.

"Oh, nothing. It's just a little gunshot wound, nothing serious. I wouldn't be wearing this damned sling but it keeps me from using the arm. I already broke the wound open once from not following doctor's orders."

"Since when did you ever follow orders?"

Cal knew Glen from the time he was a young boy living with his parents on the family farm. Glen shadowed Cal's every move while he sutured up the family dog or performed a C-section on a cow standing in a squeeze chute. He especially liked it when Doc needed an extra set of hands. Glen's family always believed he would grow up to become a veterinarian. Chances were good he'd work for Dr. Getsbowm then someday take over the practice. No one, not even Glen, had the slightest inkling he would become a top-notch detective in the big city instead. Frustrated dealing with the flaws of humanity, he often considered returning to the classroom to fulfill his early childhood dream of becoming a veterinarian.

Becky, though it took her a few seconds with his nonchalant response, couldn't help but look up when she heard Glen had been shot, arousing strong curiosity about this newcomer. Was it a bar fight? Had he been mugged? Why was everyone so calm about a man being shot?

Angie popped into the room to tell Dr. Getsbowm a cat to be neutered was prepped and on the operating table.

Clinical Death

"Well, well, if it isn't Detective Karst. What brings you here?" asked Angie.

Glen smiled at her.

"I see you're still hanging around here. How do you know I didn't come all this way just to see you?"

"Oh, give me a break." Angie, dressed in the typical attire for a rural veterinary clinic, blue jeans, t-shirt and scrub top, knocked dried manure from her boot. She moved closer to Glen, looking him squarely in the eye as she gripped his white sling between her thumb and forefinger.

"Now what'd you do?"

Before Glen could respond, Becky piped in, "He got shot."

"Again? I thought you would've learned how to dodge those bullets by now, Detective Karst," Angie teased.

Becky's nearly black eyes grew huge as she sat back staring at Glen. "Whoa. A detective," she whispered to herself.

Glen chuckled. His jovial personality allowed easy laughter, especially at himself.

"I guess maybe I'm getting too old to duck and weave the way I should."

"Yeah, right," said Angie.

She slid two chairs together, planting herself in one while pointing to the other. Glen plopped down in front of her.

"Okay, spill it Detective."

Angie wanted the entire story first hand. Small towns love scandal and the most important gossip comes directly from the source. Knowledge wields importance to the first person to attain the dirty details.

Glen, embarrassed, once again about the unwanted attention said, "There's really not much to tell. I was working a job in Omaha."

Angie cut in, " Wait a minute, Omaha? Why were you in Omaha? I thought you worked in Denver. Don't tell me you moved and we're never gonna see you again."

"Actually, I did move."

"Damn it, I knew it. You're here to say good-bye, aren't you?"

Sadness surfaced on Becky's face. She finally met her first detective, well; she hadn't exactly *met* him yet. No one formally introduced them, but at least she could *say* she met him. Now he's leaving before she could even get a chance to know him.

"That's not why I'm here. I'm here because..."

"Forget about why you're here, tell me about the gunfight."

"As I was saying..." he teased. "I was working a job in Omaha, guarding two women who were in the hospital."

Clinical Death

Angie leaned closer. "I'll bet they were beautiful, right? Had to be beautiful women to get you all the way to Omaha."

"Let him tell the story," Becky blurted out.

Glen looked up at her. His smile started a blush just above her breasts that quickly reddened her entire face.

"I don't believe we've met," said Glen. He stood to shake her hand. She extended her right hand but immediately realized his right arm was in a sling. Reaching for his left hand she then switched to her left hand, making a very awkward moment out of a simple handshake. She finally had to giggle, with the giggle she relaxed.

"Hi, I'm Becky Harrington, the new receptionist."

"Nice to meet you Becky. I'm Glen. Forgive me for not introducing myself before, too many interruptions," shooting a mischievous glance at Angie.

Angie glanced over her shoulder, knowing she should get back to work, but she really wanted this story.

"Okay, okay. Tell us what happened. I have work to do."

Glen returned to his seat. He adjusted the sling, trying not to reveal the pain he still experienced. He had a prescription but refused to use it. He felt it dulled his alertness. In his mind a cop can't exist without being totally aware of his surroundings at all times.

"It's really no big deal. The guy who tried to murder them in the first place was stalking these women. I set up a trap in their hospital room and he walked right into it. When I burst into the room to surprise him he shot me."

"Did you shoot him back?" asked Becky.

"I had no choice but to drop him," replied Glen.

"Don't be so modest," said Angie.

"What exactly do you mean by dropped him?" asked Becky.

Glen tried to think of a gentle way to phrase his next words.

"He's dead. Right, Glen?" said Angie.

He nodded.

Becky with her head upon her hands and her elbows on the counter hanging on his every word said "Wow." Then she slid quietly back into her chair.

Crime in small towns is so minimal—breaking and entering, minor vandalisms, gasoline being stolen from a farm by teenagers, but almost no violence against another person unless it's a fist fight over a girl at a party or a couple of guys over-indulging. The next day usually mends all friendships.

Detective Karst brought a piece of the real world into this small town vet clinic, touching Becky's sensitive side.

Clinical Death

"Well, I'd love to sit and chat but there's a horse out back that's ready to be castrated and Phil needs my help."

Angie gave Glen a hug before she left the room.

"Detective Karst, do you need an appointment?" asked Becky.

"Glen. Just call me Glen. I have my dog with me. She's gonna need shots and a physical. I'm thinking about breeding her."

"What breed is she?" Becky asked as she began filling out the clinic form.

"German shepherd."

"How old?"

"She's three."

"I'm sorry, I didn't ask, has she been here before?"

"Nope, I just got her. She's retired from the force with a leg injury. Actually, we've got a lot in common. She was shot, too. Her leg sustained enough damage that she'll never have the ability to run any distance on it. She made a great cop, really loved her work. They retired her before she could hurt herself, she's got a lot of heart."

"Oh, that's too bad," said Becky with a rise in the pitch of her voice. She took the job at the clinic because she loved animals and thought it would be fun to see all the puppies and kittens coming in for their first shots. She didn't realize the blood, guts and gore associated with a vet practice in the country. With no trauma centers or twenty-four hour emergency clinics, these vets treated every injury in the county. Taking turns being on call for the night shift, they were their own twenty-four hour emergency clinic.

"What's her name?"

"Mieke."

"Okay, how do you spell that?"

"M-i-e-k-e, you pronounce it Mee-kah."

Dr. Janet K. Jensen walked to the front desk to greet her next patient.

"Glen, what did you do to your arm?" she asked as she gave him a gentle hug, attempting to avoid causing him any discomfort.

"Just a scratch."

She looked at her watch.

"Do you have time to go to lunch with us?" she asked.

"I've got my dogs with me. Cheyenne rode along."

"That's okay, we can put them in a kennel. Phil should be just about done with that horse and I know Cal was finishing up on the cat. It should only be a few minutes."

Dr. Phillip E. Davis, the third veterinarian in the practice, tended to be a little more reserved than Cal or Janet. He preferred to work on horses rather than small animals.

"I'll get the girls then," said Glen.

Clinical Death

"You stay put. Becky, call Susie and Maria up front. They can get Glen's dogs and put them in a kennel in the back. Make sure they walk them first."

Susie and Maria approached the front desk. Glen tossed his keys to Susie. At first he was surprised they didn't ask about his arm but quickly realized Angie had already told them the story.

Janet slipped back down the hall to her office while Becky answered phones and set up appointments for later in the week.

Glen entertained himself wandering around the lobby checking out pet products and reading dog food bags. He wondered about diet changes for Mieke with his plans to breed her.

He read flyers from other animal owners on the bulletin board. An ad for a large black gelding caught his eye. It had been a years since he owned a horse. The urge never quite left even though he spent so many years living in the city. He made a mental note of the horses, the barn kittens and ads for puppies.

Phil and Janet walked up behind him.

Phil slapped him on the back. "Look at you. I heard you were shot."

"It's a scratch for Pete's sake," he said as he lifted his right arm away from his body. "I just wear the sling for attention."

Cal joined them. "Let's go eat. I'm hungry."

The three vets and Glen left the clinic together.

After they stepped outside, the girls who remained gathered around the front desk. They intentionally never scheduled clients during the lunch hour, allowing the vets to eat lunch together. The vets used this precious time to discuss cases and clients. However, today Glen would be their topic of discussion.

Once they placed their orders for cheeseburgers and fries, Cal turned his attention to Glen.

"I hear you moved?"

"Not quite yet, but soon. Just bought the old Watkins place."

"No shit? The city's too much for you, huh? Got shot one too many times?"

"They changed the rules and cops no longer have to live within the city limits. You all know me; I'm just a country boy at heart. I've been looking around off and on for a while now. Since Debbie and I split and put the house on the market I thought a quiet little place in the country would be perfect."

"You and Debbie split up?" asked Phil "What happened?"

Janet quickly booted him under the table and spoke up before Glen had a chance to respond.

"Tell us about your arm."

"There's not much to say. I got shot, but returned fire and sent the son of a bitch to hell."

Clinical Death

"What's this about you re-injuring your wound?" asked Cal.

"I'm not supposed to use the arm until it heals up because it tends to bleed easily. I wasn't even supposed to shift gears with it."

"Yeah, but knowing you, that didn't stop you," chided Janet, as she took a bite of her burger.

"I know you didn't damage it shifting your truck. What the hell'd you do?" asked Phil.

"I picked up more weight than I was supposed to." Glen remained evasive as he slathered ketchup and mustard over his burger.

"Look, if you don't want to tell us you don't have to," said Janet.

"Speak for yourself," said Cal. "I, for one, want to know. What'd you pick up?"

Glen set his beer down and wiped the foam from his lip.

"A woman. I carried a woman, make that two women, from a burning house."

By now the waitress had returned to listen to Glen's story. She leaned down putting her cheek next to his.

"I just have to squeeze a real hero," she said. She walked away then returned with a large piece of cheesecake smothered with cherries. She licked the sauce that dripped onto her finger.

"What's this?" asked Glen.

"I had a cheesecake in the kitchen from last night's church dinner. I planned to take it home with me tonight. But, I remembered how much you love your cheesecake. I thought after your heroic deed you deserved it."

"Hey, I saved a cow and her calf this morning," said Cal. "Isn't that heroic enough to warrant a piece of cheesecake?"

"Sorry, my husband wouldn't agree. He's expecting it for dessert tonight," the waitress replied.

"Glen, why were two women in a burning house and why were you the one to haul them out?" asked Janet.

"It's a long story. I was in Omaha working on a case. I rented a room in exchange for some carpentry work from a young widow and, long story short, she had some strange events happening in her life. I put the pieces together and arrived on the scene just as the house was about to go up in flames and carried her and one of her sisters out.

"Shortly after I carried them out I passed out from smoke inhalation and came to with an oxygen mask on my face and some paramedic trying to stop the bleeding in my arm.

"Since then, believe it or not, I've actually been trying to take care of it."

Clinical Death

Cal slid his fork gently into the edge of Glen's cheesecake slicing off a bite. "Tell us about the Watkins place."

"Not much to tell. I needed a place to live and thought it would be nice to return to my roots. It's not that long of a commute to the Denver from here. I only work four days a week and most of my research can be done from home. I get so tired of all the sheep in the city."

"Sheep? What sheep?" asked Janet.

"All the assholes who follow each other around doing the same stupid things just like a flock of sheep— bunch of damn followers."

"When are you moving in?" asked Cal.

"Next week if all goes well."

"How are you gonna move with your arm like that?" asked Janet.

"I'll manage."

"The hell you will. We'll gather a crew together and help. You just shout orders and we'll follow," said Cal.

"I can't let you guys do that."

"We didn't ask you now, did we?" said Cal.

"Where'd you get the new dog?" asked Phil, changing the subject.

"She's retired from the force. Thought I'd breed her now that I have room to have a few animals around."

Janet's cell phone disturbed their lunch conversation.

"Again? How bad is she? We'll be right there."

"What's up?" asked Phil, as he stuffed the last bit of lunch into his already full mouth.

"Ed Kurtleman brought Taffy in again. She's in pretty bad shape."

"Don't tell me she got hit by another car," said Cal.

"You guessed it."

The three vets stood to leave. Glen followed their lead leaving the rest of his lunch. He gulped his beer and carried his cheesecake out the door. In small towns no one worried the visiting cop would make away with one of their glass plates. They knew he'd return it after he washed and dried it.

Glen followed Cal and Janet into the exam room where the vet techs had already anesthetized Taffy, a sable and white Welsh Corgi, and had begun shaving her damaged leg.

Glen stepped back so as not to be in the way as he watched the crew take their places. One tech held the mask in place while the other finished shaving and scrubbing the surgery site. The x-rays of her leg were mounted on the viewing board with the lights showing the break in the leg.

Glen studied the x-ray. "What are those?" he asked, pointing to white spots in the bone of the injured leg, her hip and the other hind leg.

Cal glanced up at the x-ray.

Clinical Death

"Those are pins in her bones from previous accidents."

"Is she accident prone or just plain stupid?" asked Glen.

"Neither," said Angie. "The owner's stupid."

Janet shot her a stern look.

"Well, he is."

Janet turned to Glen.

"He's not very careful about keeping her in the yard. Her little body is so close to the ground she's hard to see when she's near a moving vehicle. Actually, it's Ed who keeps running her over. He's always in a hurry and she's anxious to ride along. If he doesn't take the time to lift her into the back of the pickup she tries to run up to it to jump in and ends up falling over and rolling under the tires."

"Crap. See what I mean about stupid people," said Glen. His heart went out to the little dog. He had a soft spot for animals. He preferred them to most people he knew.

Ed appeared at the door.

"How bad is she this time?" he asked.

"Bout the same as last time," said Janet, irritated with his lax attitude about the whole ordeal.

Glen studied the man's facial expressions, disappointed to see the lack of concern for the dog.

"This is her last time. If she gets herself into trouble again, I'm not spending another dime on her. She's pretty worthless as a cowdog now, all crippled up like that."

Angie couldn't restrain herself any longer, "Maybe you should either give away the dog or your stupid truck."

Ed pretended to ignore her. A smile crept up at the corners of Janet's mouth. She turned away from Ed so he wouldn't notice.

They finished the surgery then carried the groggy, Taffy to a kennel in the back. Ed said his good-byes and left.

"Let's take a look at your new dog," said Cal to Glen.

Angie went to the kennel to slip a leash on her. Glen was about to hoist her onto the exam table when Cal stopped him.

"Thought you weren't supposed to lift anything."

Cal slipped his arms around the chest and back legs of the German Shepherd, lifting her onto the exam table.

"What's her name?"

"Mieke."

Cal checked her heart, mouth, and ears and palpated her internal organs. "So you say you want to breed her?" he asked.

"Yeah, do you think she's in good enough health?"

Clinical Death

Cal shook down the thermometer after taking a reading.

"She's a fine animal, Glen, a fine animal. I don't see any reason why you shouldn't be able to raise some nice pups out of her."

"Great. What's next?"

"Any idea when she had her last heat cycle?"

"Sorry, no I don't."

"I'm gonna draw some blood now and run a fecal and do a vaginal swab. Why don't you give us a call tomorrow or stop by and I'll let you know if we find anything."

"That'll be great."

Susie hurried into the room. "Cal, George Peterson called. He's got a horse down with colic."

Cal washed his hands then rushed out the door with Susie to drive to George's farm.

Angie and Becky helped Glen load his dogs and he headed back to Denver.

Midmorning the next day, Glen stopped by the clinic. He'd been to his new place making plans for the move.

"Morning, Detective Karst," said Becky.

"Glen."

"Oops. Sorry, Glen. What can I do for you?"

"I'm here for the test results for Mieke."

Becky left the front desk to find a vet or tech who could give Glen the answers he needed.   Angie followed her to the front.

"Doc says she's fine," said Angie.

"Great." Glen turned to leave. "Say, how's that little dog, Taffy?"

"She's doing better than her owner," said Angie.

"Why do you say that?"

"He was found dead this morning."

"Jesus. What happened?"

Had they been in the city Glen wouldn't have been surprised, but things like this don't happen often in the country.

"Not sure. His neighbor found him under his truck. He must've been checking something underneath and it rolled over the top of him. Pinned under the tire they say. One of the neighbors stopped by to talk to him when he didn't show up at the coffee shop this morning. I told him he should'a got rid of that truck."

Chapter 2

Glen's self-imposed assignment in Omaha cost him his position with the Denver department. They gave him fair warning, but dedication to protecting his friend, mystery writer Maggi Morgan, surpassed the desire to remain in good standing with his job. Upon his return to Denver he made an appointment to visit with his sergeant. His outstanding performance on the job allowed his sergeant to reinstate him.

They both agreed to wait until his arm healed adequately enough to drive easily. Being right-handed handicapped him in the event he needed to use his gun, though he was still proficient with his left hand. The time off fit perfectly into Glen's current life. He needed to sell the Denver home and move to his new place. He could use the extra free time having signed the papers on the old Watkins farm.

Years ago, when he left to pursue his career in law enforcement, he never dreamed he would return to

Wallace, Colorado. Only thirty minutes northeast of Denver, the small town setting proved to be the perfect escape for him. Too bad his old friend and partner, Dave, was no longer alive. He would've been amused that Glen finally took his advice to move to a quieter part of the world. Dave relocated to Holyoke, Colorado a number of years ago, before his untimely death.

His move to small town living allowed him the benefit of both worlds.

As Glen left the vet clinic that morning he drew a deep breath—no exhaust fumes and no rush of traffic. He and the dogs drove along the highway toward his new farm. South of town, he rolled down the windows to smell the freshly tilled soil. Farmers worked their fields from early in the morning until late in the evening. The weather always kept them pushing ahead at a rapid speed to beat the next rain, which would make the fields too muddy to work. Timing is everything for a good crop. Farmers tend to get cranky when they can't plant or harvest their crops in a timely manner.

As they drove closer to his turn the dogs barked excitedly at the sight and smell of cattle grazing in the pastures. Along the edge of the dirt road stood a worn mailbox mounted on a piece of irrigation pipe. The weatherworn name read, K U R T L E M A N. Glen pulled over.

Clinical Death

"Son of a bitch," he murmured. "That stupid bastard was my neighbor." He pulled into the driveway to take a look around. The old worn out farmhouse desperately needed a coat of new paint. The barns, with broken windows and rotted boards, stood as a symbol of a huge farming operation of the past. He admired the old milking barn, the stable for horses and the smaller pig and chicken buildings. It reminded him of his boyhood days. Although his parents had downsized tremendously, they still managed to keep enough livestock around to provide an income as well as food for the family.

His dad and granddad always said, "Hard work will make a man out of you."

As a boy he thought, even without the hard work, he'd still grow into manhood, but now he understood exactly what they meant. Working a farm and taking care of livestock taught responsibility and respect for life and death. Farm kids learned about death early on.

Ed's truck remained parked near the shop building where all types of repairs took place. Glen stopped his pickup and got out. The girls wanted to join him but he told them to stay put. He didn't know if Ed lived alone and surely didn't want his dogs to play chase with someone else's cats or chickens.

Glen's eyes scanned the ground for evidence of a crime. He couldn't help himself; it was second nature. He wondered how difficult it might be to turn off his city instincts or the reverse, what if living in the country dulled his urban senses? He studied the marks in the soil near the truck. He could tell by the roughed up soil which tire Ed had been pinned under. There was evidence of other people around the spot, probably the neighbors and paramedics.

Something seemed odd. The powder dry soil mixed with gravel bits was level. Why would the truck move forward or backward on level ground? Even if the pickup had been idling, there would be no cause for it to move. Cheyenne distracted Glen when she began to whine at the sight of a barn cat playing with a mouse.

Glen returned to his pickup and drove down the road to his own little slice of heaven.

His new house, although old, had been very well cared for. It appeared to have been remodeled in the late seventies or early eighties. With his keen carpenter skills he could quickly make the changes needed to personalize it. Right now it required nothing but his possessions. The family he purchased it from had hired a cleaning crew before listing it on the market. The local realtor said he was the first person to inquire. The farmland surrounding the house had numerous neighbors interested. Glen decided to allow the farming to continue on a cash lease. The small extra income could help to pay the loan off sooner. The realtor had a number of farmers lined up to

Clinical Death

speak with Glen for the next farming season. This year's crops had already been contracted.

As he wandered through the house he felt anxious to move in. His arm stuck in a sling put a damper on that. He secretly hoped his friends at the vet clinic would follow through with their promise to help him.

His first order of business would be to repair the fence in the backyard and install a doggie door. There was a nice mud-porch in the back of the house quite suitable for the dogs. They could have shelter when needed while having free access to the yard. Feeling slightly agitated by his immobility he decided to drive back into town for groceries. At least he could carry bags one-handed and stock the kitchen.

All eyes scrutinized the handsomely rugged detective dressed like a cowboy. His black duster whooshed with each step. His boots clicked on the tile floor as he pushed the cart along the aisles. He searched for the liquor section, discovering it to be non-existent. He bought three steaks, one for him and one for each of the dogs to celebrate their new home. He stocked up on breakfast supplies, plenty of meat to grill, the basics in condiments, but the basket lacked vegetables except for a couple cans of beans.

Across the street from the grocery store he located his favorite brand of bourbon, Buffalo Trace. Life was now complete, finding the peace and quiet of a small town plus his preferred liquor. He returned to the farmhouse and lit the charcoal in the brick grill in the backyard. He and the dogs explored while they waited for the coals to turn white.

Inside the barn he found empty dog food bags stacked neatly in the corner. The stalls had been altered with chicken wire to hold small animals. He found water bowls still containing water. His eyes noticed rectangular impressions in the soft powdery dirt of the stalls. The pattern reminded him of the bottom of the plastic dog kennels he had for his dogs.

Cheyenne and Mieke were fascinated with the smells. They sniffed every inch of the stalls. Cheyenne dug in the dirt until she uncovered a dog toy. Glen called her.

"Let me see that," he said as he removed it from her mouth. The bright red stuffed toy showed no signs of deterioration. The white tag told Glen the toy was nearly brand new.

Mieke bounced up to him dropping a new tennis ball at his feet, hoping he would play fetch with her. Normally, he would have thrown it hard and far but with her injured leg he tossed it gently across the barn where it sent a puff of dust into the air.

He started back to the house to check on the coals when the two dogs raced past him and disappeared behind the barn. He went to see what they were up to.

Clinical Death

There he found them sniffing around a pile of dog manure. The mound looked as though someone had been discarding it there for a long time, but the piles on top were still fresh. Someone had recently been living there with what appeared to be a large number of dogs. Upon closer examination he discerned the dogs were of various sizes.

Glen's steak was grilled to perfection. The girls ate theirs raw. Glen enjoyed his meal of grilled steak, baked beans and a large hunk of French bread slathered with butter. Time had slipped away this morning and he didn't realize how hungry he was until he started to eat.

As he loaded the dishes into the dishwasher his cell phone rang. He quickly dried his hands and grabbed it from the kitchen counter.

"Glen here."

"Glen, this is Larona. I'm calling to see if everything is okay with your house."

"Absolutely," said Glen.

Larona worked for the local real estate office. She made purchasing the farm a snap.

"Good. I'm glad. Let me know if you need anything."

"Thanks, I will. Say, how long did you say it's been since someone lived here?"

"Oh dear, did you find a mouse or snake or something? That can happen when a house sits vacant too long. The wildlife thinks it's theirs to take over."

"No, nothing like that. The cleaning crew did a great job. No critters in the house, but there were signs..." Glen hesitated. His detective instincts told him not to give out information but rather to collect it. He continued, "There were signs that there must've been lots of animals living here at one time when the farm was active."

"Yes, you're quite right. It was a pretty busy place in its day. Let's see, you wanted to know how long since anyone actually lived there. My file says it's been seventeen years. The old Watkins couple moved into town and wouldn't rent it out. Then their grandkids would come stay once in a while in the summer months. But now it looks as though no one has been staying there for at least the past twelve years. Is there a problem?"

"No. No problem. I'm just interested in the history of the place. I don't remember the Watkins family. I noticed there are *no hunting* signs posted everywhere on the property. Do you think the hunters take them seriously or do they tend to make themselves at home when they run across an abandoned farm like this?"

"No. Not to my knowledge. The hunters we get here have been pretty good about minding their manners. Sheriff Tate does a pretty good job of keeping an eye on them during the season. Is there anything else?"

Clinical Death

"No, but hey, thanks for calling to check on me."

Glen went out to the porch swing since the house was void of furniture. He swung both legs up onto the swing as he sat sideways propelling the swing into a slow, swaying motion. He stroked his chin with his left hand as he contemplated the conversation.

Someone's been here with dogs recently. No sign anyone broke into the house or has been living here, but why would someone keep dogs here? He thought about the barn. The chicken wire, feedbags and the bowls with standing water in them told him someone moved the animals out in a big hurry. He considered dusting the bags for fingerprints then chuckled to himself. No harm's been done; give it a break old man.

The dogs barking caused Glen to look up. He saw a white pickup pulling into the yard. He stood from the swing to greet his first guests. Janet and Cal stepped out.

"Thought we'd find you here," said Cal.

" Great to see you guys. What's up?"

"We've got a crew of a dozen people to help with the move. How's Saturday afternoon sound?" responded Cal.

"Great. I can't believe you guys're doing this. You didn't need to drive all the way out here to tell me. You could've called. I gave Becky my cell phone number."

"We had to stop by Kurtleman's to check on a cow that got herself tangled up in some barbed wire. So we thought we'd stop by to see if you were home," said Janet.

"Now you do know you have to supply all the burgers and dogs and beer the moving crew can devour."

"That's a deal. How's the cow?"

"Nasty cut on her hind leg. We got her out of the pasture and into the corral. Ed's loading chute is in pretty sorry shape, but we ran her in and cleaned the wound. We shot her up with antibiotics. She nearly kicked my head off when I reached down to take the wire off. Can't believe how they can still manage to get body parts out of the chute when they want to," said Cal.

"Did you hear about Ed?" Janet asked.

"Yeah, the girls at the clinic told me this morning when I stopped in. I had no idea he was my neighbor until I saw his name on the mailbox. Did you find out any more about his death?"

"Not much," said Janet. "I guess he was pretty loaded and crawled under his pickup to check something. Must've been bad timing or something. Poor Ed. What a terrible way to die."

"Hell, he was probably so drunk he had no idea he was in pain," said Cal.

"You know, I stopped by there this morning and checked out the spot where I think it happened. Kind of odd that his pickup rolled on flat ground."

Cal slapped Glen on the back. "Keep your detecting skills to the city, man. We don't want everyone here looking over their shoulder all the time scaring the hell out of each other with gossip."

"Farm accidents happen all the time, Glen. No need to worry yourself about them. It's just part of life out here," said Janet.

"That's right," said Cal. "What was it, about a month ago? Clyde Malcolm drowned in his irrigation ditch. Just like Ed, he didn't show up for coffee and the guys started talking about him. They called his cell phone and got no answer. They called his wife and she thought he'd left early for town and had no idea where he was. She went out to look for him around the place and couldn't find him. Then one of the locals found his pickup near the irrigation ditch. Found him floating on top of the water face down."

"How do you suppose that happened?" asked Glen.

"Doc said he must've had a heart attack and stumbled into the water," said Janet.

"What'd the autopsy report say?"

"Hell, Glen. There wasn't any autopsy. Most folks around here don't bother. Why throw the money away, it ain't gonna bring anybody back to life?" said Cal.

"I know, but aren't they curious about foul play?"

"Glen, there hasn't been a murder here in over one hundred years," laughed Cal. "Man, if you're gonna fit in here you really gotta stop playing Dick Tracy and spend more time smellin' the wildflowers."

Glen didn't respond. His instincts told him this town probably let crimes pass while not even realizing they were crimes. Could he really live here or would they run him out for starting trouble?

"Well," started Janet. "We'd better get going or they'll wonder what happened to us. Guess we'll see you on Saturday."

Glen waved as they drove off, "See ya Saturday."

He ran his fingers through his hair the way he did when something bothered him. Sometimes he wondered if having worked with the psychic, Jennifer Parker, on past cases had caused him to misinterpret random thoughts as intuition or gut instincts. She convinced him he had abilities he had not even tapped into yet.

He went into the kitchen to fill his glass with bourbon and return to the swing. He thought back to when his gut instincts told him to run as far away from Jennifer Parker as possible. But damn, she helped him find that little girl and even taught him how to go within himself to find answers. He remembered his first vision with the train tracks.

He sipped his bourbon; pondering the time Jennifer saved his life when he'd been shot in the head. No, she'd been right on with too many cases; he had to give her the benefit of the doubt.

Maybe he should go back to work. He's only been at his new place for a few hours and already he's discovered someone secretly boarding dogs on his place and two deaths he's ready to turn into homicide investigations. Years ago he made a promise to himself to never become complacent, it's all about balance and he had to make it work.

He returned to Denver to finish packing. At least he should be able to keep himself busy carrying his clothes on hangers and in suitcases. His personality wouldn't let him sit idle while he waited for others to come by and do all of the work.

On one of his numerous trips to the pickup carrying what his one arm would allow, his cell phone rang. Partway between the house and the pickup, with his only functioning hand occupied, he had no choice but to ignore the ring. After placing his clothes in the backseat he checked the phone. It was Bill, his partner at the time he quit the department.

"Bill, Glen here. Sorry I missed your call; I had my hands full. What's up?"

"I heard through the grapevine you talked your way back in. You slick son of a bitch, I'm not sure how you managed that one."

"I think Sarge understood the dilemma I was faced with, that's all."

"So, do ya think he'll team us up again?"

"I don't know, he didn't say."

"Everyone's talking about you getting shot again."

"Jesus, why does everyone have to add that *again* to it?"

"What?"

"Oh nothing. Yeah, I got shot but I'm walking around. The bastard who shot me isn't so lucky. Did you pass that on?"

"When are you starting back? Today maybe?"

"Nah, I'm gonna wait until my arm's healed. What's happening today that has you so uptight?"

"There's this old lady that died in her sleep and some of her friends don't think it happened that way."

Glen sat on the tailgate to continue the conversation.

"Why? What do they think happened?"

"Seems her nephew was in a hurry to collect his inheritance but the old lady wasn't dying fast enough to suit him. Or so she told her friends. She thought he'd try to kill her."

"Did he?"

"Shit, I dunno. I'm on my way over there right now. Wanna come along?"

"I'm not on the payroll yet."

"That's okay. Just take a look at the scene and let me know what you think."

"She's still there?"

"Yeah."

Clinical Death

Glen jotted down the address. He closed up the house and put the dogs in the backyard. When he arrived at the scene, everyone had a fairly casual attitude except for three gray-haired women who appeared to be all worked up.

Bill walked up to Glen. "The old lady's still in her bed. When her housekeeper came in to work this morning she found her. She called her friends first, then the nephew then 911."

"Why didn't she call 911 first?"

"She said the woman had apparently been dead for some time. She was cold. The old lady told her to call her friends first if anything happened to her. She took it upon herself to call the nephew. He told her to call 911."

"Have you been inside yet?"

"No," said Bill. "I got here just before you pulled in."

"Let's check it out," said Glen.

As they walked up to the porch one of the ladies grabbed Glen's good arm.

"Are you going to arrest him? He killed Evelyn you know."

"Ma'am, I'm not sure what's going to happen. I need to do my job now. I'll talk with you very soon, okay?"

Glen stopped for a moment inside to appreciate the architectural design of this beautiful old home in Cherry Creek. He ran his fingers along the ornately carved woodwork. Sliding his hand along the wide oak railing curving along the stairs, he noticed a chairlift had been installed.

He ran up the stairs two at a time to join Bill. Inside the master bedroom lay a fragile little woman wearing a pink nightgown and robe. Her matching slippers were on the floor near the bed.

When the paramedics telephoned the on-call physician explaining the condition of the body he pronounced her dead. The coroner's investigator was snapping photographs. The scene appeared as nothing more than an elderly woman who died in her sleep.

Her nephew arrived. He tried to rush in past the officers at the door to the bedroom who stopped him. He dropped to his knees sobbing. Glen approached and touched him on the shoulder.

"Who are you?" he asked.

"She's my aunt."

"I'm sorry for your loss. Why don't you wait downstairs until we finish up here."

Glen motioned for one of the uniformed officers to take him downstairs. The women's accusations turned what most would consider a peaceful death into something of suspicion.

Clearance had been given to remove the body.

"Wait. Can you give us a minute?" asked Glen.

Clinical Death

Bill looked up from his notepad. How well he knew that look on Glen's face.

Bill said, "Okay, everybody. Clear out."

One by one, the crime scene investigators filed out the door.

Glen checked the hall to be absolutely certain the nephew had not sneaked back upstairs.

"What?" asked Bill.

"Lots," said Glen.

Bill flipped his notepad open again. Glen wasn't officially on the case. Bill sent the others away so no one would know who had the hunches, Glen or Bill.

"When I was downstairs I was admiring the workmanship on the stair railing when I noticed the chairlift. Do you know if anyone touched anything after her death?"

"No, according to the cleaning lady. She found her, went down to the kitchen, made the calls and waited outside."

"Don't you think it's a bit odd that this immobile woman left her wheelchair in the downstairs living room and not at the base of the stairs where the lift is? Also, if no one touched anything since she put herself to bed last night then why was the lift at the bottom of the stairs? How did she manage to get up here? Her other wheelchair is still at the top of the stairs where the lift would've dropped her off," said Glen.

"Son of a bitch. Your vacation time has been good to you. You're right. If she was wheelchair bound, how the hell did she get up those stairs?"

Glen went on.

"Also, check out her slippers."

"What about them?"

"Unless someone kicked them around this morning they look tossed. Don't you imagine a woman like this would have sat on the edge of the bed, probably with her feet together and slid her feet out of the slippers? And, why would she sleep with her robe on?"

Bill surveyed the situation as Glen talked. It's possible one of the points Glen mentioned could have happened, but not all of them, especially the part about the chairlift.

Glen walked over to her bed table. On the table, opposite the side of the bed where the body was found, sat a carved crystal bowl with a lid. Glen took his pen from his pocket to lift the lid.

"Now what?" asked Bill.

"Check this out. The lady wears dentures. She stores them here at night. Why would she climb into a large bed and have to crawl across it to reach the table on the other side to place her teeth in the bowl?"

"Damn, someone else put this vic to bed."

"Exactly my thoughts," said Glen. "Someone else carried her body up the stairs, so she didn't need the wheelchairs or lift. Whoever it was slipped her into the bed, carelessly pulled off her slippers and tossed them on the floor, left her dentures in and tucked her in on the wrong side of the bed."

Bill called on his radio, "Send the housekeeper up here."

Bill and Glen met Susanne in the hall so she wouldn't have to experience her discovery again.

Bill took over the questioning.

"Good morning, Susanne. I'm so sorry you had to see this. I'll make my questions quick. Could Mrs. Montgomery walk without her wheelchair?"

"Not very well. She could stand briefly, but her legs were too shaky to hold her up. She could take care of herself as long as she had her wheelchairs. She was a proud woman and didn't want a nurse."

"Did Mrs. Montgomery wear dentures?"

"Yes, she kept them in the crystal bowl beside her bed at night."

"Did you touch her when you found her?"

"No."

"Was she sleeping on her usual side?"

"Now that you mention it," replied Susanne. "No, she always slept on the other side to be closer to the bathroom."

"Thanks, I might want to talk to you again to learn more about Mrs. Montgomery."

Bill called downstairs, "Is the nephew still here?"

"Yeah. Do you want to see him?" asked the voice on the radio.

"No. Just make sure he doesn't leave."

Chapter 3

Glen's instincts were stronger than ever. Maybe Bill was right; time off cleared his head and allowed him to catch up on much needed sleep.

He spent the remainder of the week packaging small items and taping boxes. One's ability to perform minor household duties with one arm grows stronger each day as improvisational skills surface.

Strong muscular legs were a gift that likely came from skiing since he was two years old. Russian martial arts most of his adult life kept them toned. Unable to lift the boxes, he scooted them along the floor using his legs. By Friday Glen managed to move most of the contents of the house into the living room making it easier for his volunteer crew.

Daily he and the dogs made trips with the smaller items. He purchased lots of groceries to feed his help. One day while unloading them, he realized how easy items were to carry when they were in plastic bags. He gathered the bags, taking them back to the house creating a method to carry multiple items with one arm.

Friday night he and the dogs stayed at the farmhouse. Glen slept in a sleeping bag with the dogs curled tightly next to him. The cool country air wafted in through the kitchen windows mixing with the aroma of brewing coffee. Glen tore open a package of sweet rolls to eat with his coffee.

Barefoot and without a shirt, Glen sat on the porch swing sipping his coffee and eating rolls. With the sleeping bag wrapped around his shoulders, he listened to the calls of birds. The smell of spring filled the air. Tulips and daffodils were dropping their blooms as the sweetrocket sprouts shot up along the house soon to release their nighttime perfume into the air. He wondered why he ever abandoned the country life.

The dogs bounced off of the porch barking at the parade of trucks and stock trailers approaching the house. Glen whistled for them to return. Not expecting his help so early in the morning, he jumped up from the swing tangled in the sleeping bag cord spilling coffee on his bare foot.

"Shit," he said as he danced instinctively when the hot coffee scalded his skin.

Cal was the first to reach the porch.

"Hey, the city boy's not up and ready to go. Half the day's gone by."

Clinical Death

"Guess I forgot you guys still get up with the chickens out here," said Glen.

"Literally," said Angie. "Speaking of chickens, that's a great chicken house. You gonna get some?"

Glen looked across the farmyard at the chicken house. The thought of chickens hadn't crossed his mind.

"Doubtful. I'll have to think about it."

"I'm sure these guys would love some fresh caught chicken in the mornings," said Cal as he ruffled the fur around the heads of the two shepherds.

"Come on in. I'll just be a minute," said Glen.

"No, that's okay," Janet replied. "We'll just wait outside."

All three vets, their techs and the two receptionists with their husbands waited patiently for Glen.

Glen put the dogs inside, slipped into a shirt and tugged on his boots. He grabbed his hat and joined the others in the front yard, counting heads.

"Hell, how much stuff do you think a bachelor has?"

"The way I look at it," said Phil, stroking his dark mustache. "The more people we have, the less work any one of us will have to do. You did remember the food, didn't you?"

"Oh yeah. Does anyone want coffee or pop or anything before we get started?" asked Glen.

"Nope. Let's get the show on the road," said Janet. She knew her husband had plans for the two of them later in the day.

Glen gave everyone the address and his cell phone number then they followed him thirty miles southwest to Denver.

The cluster of boxes Glen had spent the week gathering soon disappeared. The men carried furniture out while the women held doors and arranged boxes inside the stock trailers. Glen handcrafted much of furniture and he cringed at the thought of someone being careless, but resigned himself to stand back and let them work.

"Bet you're glad we washed the shit out of the trailers before we came," teased Angie.

"Good morning, Becky," said Glen as she walked past him carrying a box.

She blushed, "Good morning Detective...er, Glen."

Glen smiled at her shyness, a trait he himself never experienced.

In less than an hour the entire house and garage were empty. Soon they were back at the farm unloading. Glen brewed more coffee.

"There's beer and pop in the refrigerator, help yourself," he said. "Remember, beer is for drinking while you're working but bourbon is for relaxing when the work is done."

Clinical Death

He noticed the women cutting open the boxes with pocketknives.

"Hey, I can do that. You guys have already done too much."

"Just shut up and go join the rest of the guys," said Angie.

Susie and Maria, the two more reserved vet techs, found the boxes of linens and made the beds. Then they put away the towels. Angie and Janet finished the kitchen. Glen had already moved most of the kitchen items during the week. When he went through the house to get more beer for the men he noticed the nearly empty boxes. The women had really rolled up their sleeves and gone to work. He felt hotdogs and burgers wouldn't be enough to repay them. Then his eyes caught sight of a platter holding one large cheesecake. Next to the cheesecake was a bottle of Buffalo Trace Bourbon with a big red bow.

"What's this?" asked Glen, feeling even more embarrassed.

"Oh, that's your housewarming gift. The cheesecake is from the ladies and the booze is from the guys. Welcome to the community," said Janet.

Glen gave Janet a big hug. She was one sturdy woman. But you wouldn't know that to look at her. She stood five-foot-five and weighed about one hundred and fifty pounds but when he squeezed her he felt her muscular body squeeze back. No wonder she could handle the large animal side of their vet practice so well. He smiled when he considered the high maintenance city women who have their sights set on him. He preferred attractive countrywomen who could shoot, cook, help with the livestock and still knock your socks off in lingerie.

"Here, let me take those," said Janet as she took the bottles from Glen. "I'll check to see if those guys are ready to start the grill."

Alone with Angie, Glen wondered how much information he could draw out of her without her becoming suspicious.

"Hey, I heard some guy named Malcolm died last month," he said.

"Oh, Clyde? Yeah, he drowned. Heart attack by the water."

"Was he married?"

"Yeah. His wife's really sweet."

"How's she getting along without him? I'll bet it's pretty rough."

"Not too bad. She has three grown boys. They'd been farming with their dad part time so they were able to help her out. She might give up the farm to one of them and move into town."

"Who are you guys talking about?" Janet interrupted.

Clinical Death

"Agnes," said Angie. "I was just telling Glen how she might move into town."

"Sweet lady. I hope now that he's gone she can get some of those cats neutered," said Janet.

"She likes cats, huh?" asked Glen, trying to make conversation when his concern was more about her husband's death.

"Man, does she ever. Clyde couldn't stand them. Every time one of them spit out a litter of kittens he'd drown them. Poor Agnes would cry for days. She wanted to have the mother cats spayed but he refused to put the money into worthless barn cats.

"One time," said Janet, "he showed up at the clinic with this homemade cage contraption in the back of his pickup filled with adult cats. He wanted to drop them off at the clinic so we'd find homes for them. I told him we weren't set up for that. He drove home and tossed the cage and all into the irrigation ditch."

"Maybe the ghosts of all those cats came up out of the water and pulled him in," said Angie, as she twisted and contorted her face into how she thought an angry cat ghost would appear.

For the next two hours the group sat on Glen's porch eating and drinking. Cal told them stories of Glen as a boy. Soon they were gone as quickly as they had arrived that morning. His first party and the guests had cleaned everything up before they left. He slipped into the kitchen for a glass of bourbon and a stroll through his house to see how it looked with all the furnishings.

The following Monday Glen kept his doctor appointment in Denver to check on the progress of his arm.

"I don't believe it," said the doctor.

"What? What's wrong?" asked Glen, concerned he may be stuck with the sling longer than planned.

"I don't believe it, you actually followed orders. The wound looks good. I think we can do away with the sling. Go ahead and start using it but don't lift more than five or ten pounds with it. If it hurts or starts to ooze, stop using it for a few more days."

"When can I go back to work?"

"How does next week sound?"

"Dandy."

"Now, remember just because I'm giving you the green light doesn't mean life as normal. Let's avoid a few bullets and none of that martial arts stuff on the bad guys. Try to spend as much time as possible at your desk in the beginning."

The doctor knew his words fell upon deaf ears, but he felt it his duty as a medical professional to at least try.

Glen smiled, thinking the Russian style martial arts made a one-armed man more formidable than a very skilled two-armed opponent.

Clinical Death

On his way home, Glen stopped by the vet clinic to drop off the cheesecake platter. He and his guests made short order of it, leaving only a few slices for him to enjoy.

All hell broke loose when he showed up at the clinic without his sling. Everyone teased him about faking it to get them to do all the work of moving him. He wandered around the clinic as he visited with each of the vets.

Taffy was on an exam table while Phil and Susie checked her leg.

"Hey, that's my neighbor's dog. How's she doing?" Glen put his hand under her chin, raising her face up to look into her eyes as he patted her on the head.

"She's doing fine," said Susie with tears welling in her eyes.

"What's wrong?" Glen asked.

"Ed's only family is his brother, Neal from Wisconsin. When he came for Ed's funeral I asked him what he wanted to do with the dog and the cattle," said Phil as he stroked his mustache, a habit he had when he was talking. "He said to run the cattle through the sale barn, put the dog to sleep and he'd hire someone to do the farming."

Glen looked into the big brown eyes of the little dog as she wagged her tail and licked his fingers. Susie left the room crying.

"She's too soft-hearted for this job. She'll never last," said Phil.

"Can't you find a home for her?" asked Glen.

"Oh, we'll keep her around for a week or so, but that'd be going against the wishes of her new so-called owner."

"How's she doing health wise?" asked Glen.

"She's a tough little girl. A few more weeks and I expect she'll be good as new on this leg, just like with all of her other injuries."

Glen scooped her up into his arms. She smothered his face with kisses.

"She's coming home with me," said Glen.

"Now, don't let Susie get to you. That's just part of the business. Occasionally, we do have to destroy animals," said Phil.

"I know. It's not Susie. It's these big brown eyes. Besides, Mieke needs someone to play with since Cheyenne's too old."

Glen walked into the front lobby carrying Taffy. Susie was off in the corner trying to regain her composure.

"What are you doing with Taffy?" asked Stacey. She worked as a receptionist with Becky. She'd been there for almost twenty years. Her big blue eyes and chubby face always lit up when Glen appeared. Along with most other women, she secretly had a crush on him.

Clinical Death

His soft green eyes and sandy brown hair gave a gentle touch to the rugged self-assured detective.

"I'm taking her home. I think the girls and I can find room for her. Maybe she can teach my two city dogs how to live in the country."

Susie bounded from behind the desk throwing her arms around Glen's neck, squeezing until she nearly choked him. She pulled back, embarrassed, when she realized what she'd done. He slipped his arm around her waist to return the hug and ease her discomfort over her reaction to the news. Glen could not quite figure out what made being a detective so romantic to some women, but he found himself constantly in situations where women slipped him their phone numbers or email addresses.

Glen introduced Cheyenne and Mieke to Taffy. He made her a bed on the mud porch, confining her area as Phil instructed. He patted her on the head. "I know how tough it is to feel restricted," he told her as he rubbed his arm.

He called Larona to inquire about Ed's farm.

"Larona, Glen. I'm fine. Yes, my arm's better."

He found it difficult to get a word in. Finally she paused.

He took advantage of the quiet moment, "Larona, what's going to happen to the farm next door to me?"

"Ed's place?"

"Yes."

"Nothing for the moment. Ed's brother says he doesn't want it rented out or sold. The boys were raised there and even though he never comes back here, he wants to hold on to it. Why? Did you want to add it to your property?"

"No, I just wanted to know who my new neighbors would be."

"Sorry, Glen. You're gonna be all alone on that stretch of road. No neighbors within three miles."

"Don't be sorry. I like the privacy."

He couldn't shake that feeling about the apparent accident next door. Now he felt he had the opportunity to snoop around when the urge hit him. No need to share his findings with anyone because no one wanted to admit a crime could have been committed. The case closed when Ed was buried. Some cases Glen couldn't let rest and he wondered if this would be one of them.

The following Monday, Glen showed up for work carrying boxes of donuts. His co-workers pretended they were happier to see the donuts than him. Forced to repeat his story about being shot more times than he cared to made for a nonproductive morning.

Bill stopped by his desk to grab a donut and welcome him back.

"Any word yet about who you'll be working with?" he asked.

Clinical Death

"For a while I'm glued to the desk. I'm pretty sure you're gonna be stuck with me when I'm no longer cuffed to this damn computer."

"Forget the computer, check out your basket. I've been tossing files in there hoping you'd get back to work soon. The hours here have been hell. Must be something in the air. We've got more missing persons and homicides than we can handle. Sarge told us to get through the easy ones first to bring the numbers down, but we still have a shitload of tough cases."

"Speaking of cases, what became of the Montgomery woman and her nephew?" asked Glen.

"Hey, thanks for that one. I got to take credit for your sleuthing. Anyway, I ordered an autopsy. The nephew put up a fight at first but he backed down when I put a little pressure on him. The old dame showed signs of petechial hemorrhaging."

"No shit," said Glen. "The little bastard smothered her, huh?"

"Turns out he kept running to her for money until finally she got tired of giving it to him. His parents died when he was a kid. She took care of him and was left in charge of his parent's money. After he grew up and moved away he blew his allowance. Bombed out of school because he partied too much. When he started gambling with a bookie, she shut him off.

"Her friends were right. He was a loser and she knew he'd try to kill her."

Bill sorted through the donuts, finding his favorite cherry-filled with white icing.

"You get enough for a conviction?"

"Son of a bitch," said Bill. He had bitten into the donut dripping jelly down the front of his shirt. "What'd you say?"

"Do you have enough to try him?"

"Don't need to," he said as he tried wiping the jelly off his shirt with a flimsy napkin leaving bits of white paper on the stain.

Glen waited until Bill stopped fidgeting with his jelly-stained shirt.

"The little weenie confessed. I could tell when he backed down so easy about the autopsy that he didn't have a spine. I told him his aunt had been strangled and we knew he did it. I reconstructed the crime scene right up to the bowl for the dentures. I did thank you for that one, didn't I? Anyway, I stretched the facts a bit to include a witness seeing his car drive away that night."

"There was no witness, was there?" asked Glen.

"No. But once he felt backed into a corner he confessed. So I have a signed statement and the puke's going to prison for offing his aunt."

Clinical Death

Glen opened his desk drawer. He took out a water bottle and a clean handkerchief. He handed them both to Bill so he could clean his shirt.

Nothing had changed. Bill, still overweight and overbearing, lacked persuasive charm both with the ladies and with suspects. Glen thought back to how Maggi Morgan put him in his place when he came on to her. Bill should have known with Maggi's looks she wouldn't give someone like him the time of day. Ironically, Maggi turned to Bill for help when Glen was in Omaha, which ultimately developed into a healthy respect for each other.

Glen spent the next few hours reviewing and prioritizing the cases on his desk.

"What the hell has everyone been doing around here?" he mumbled.

Eventually, he had three stacks of files before him: now, later and fill. The now stack contained the cases that bothered him—something just wasn't right. Later were cases with either legitimate explanations or absolutely no leads. Fill were cases he could resolve with little effort, saved for the times the division needed clearance numbers.

"No wonder my sergeant loves me," he chuckled.

Glen took the top folder from his now stack; he read the report. Christine Slater, 43 years old, mother of four—missing. Christine worked in a high paying position as a stockbroker. She had three girls, one boy, and a husband, Frank Slater. According to the interviewing officer, the husband reported a happy marriage with no reason for her sudden disappearance. On the morning of February twentieth she missed work. Co-workers called her cell phone. When there was no answer, they called her husband. He stated she left for work at the same time she did every morning. He had no idea where she might be.

The next day she remained missing. Her husband and friends checked all her contacts. Christine's family had not heard from her. Her mother said Christine was a good mom and would never have left her kids.

Glen glanced at the top of the report to see when the husband had called in. To his surprise, he discovered it was her co-workers who had called the police. He made a mental note of that interesting piece of information.

He decided to begin with the co-workers. He jotted down the address of her brokerage firm, grabbed the folder and his badge and was back on the job. One by one, he interviewed her colleagues. They told him the same story. Christine took her work seriously, rarely missing a day.

However, one of them did make a strange comment. She said, "Christine told us if anything ever happened to her that her life story is in her work, whatever that means."

Clinical Death

Glen requested access to the missing woman's office. He searched through her desk. In one of the drawers under a stack of papers he discovered a legal pad with a partially written letter to her husband. She expressed her unhappiness and wanted out of the marriage. He sat at the computer to check her emails. Fortunately for him, a password was not necessary to gain access. His search led him to nearly a dozen men with whom she'd been emailing for the past three years.

He printed one email from each man. Next he needed to match the email addresses to names, photos and physical addresses. Each of these men would be suspect until proven otherwise. The husband is always first on the list of suspects in the beginning, but it appeared to him as though Christine may have met the wrong person online. Or, he thought, maybe she met Mr. Right and happily walked away from her present life into the arms of another man.

Two and a half weeks later Glen had located and interviewed each of the men. Each had a viable alibi. His gut told him while he visited with them he was not sitting face to face with a killer. His thoughts returned to the husband.

He met with Frank Slater expressing his heartfelt condolences for his loss and complimented his strength in such a dire situation. They spoke for more than an hour under the guise that Glen wanted to learn more about

Christine to gain focus for his investigation. Glen listened, more importantly watched, as Frank repeatedly failed to show remorse when Glen slipped in his innuendos of Christine's possible death. Otherwise, Frank did an excellent job of appearing distraught, but Glen still had enough to doubt his integrity and innocence. Frank eventually and reluctantly admitted to Christine's intention to leave him.

Glen used Christine's letter and various tidbits from the interview as probable cause to obtain a search warrant for Slater's home and office computers. He wasn't certain what he was looking for.

While he visited with the man, he detected his uneasiness. The way he avoided eye contact with Glen, the way he squirmed in the chair, the way he clicked the pen in his hand nervously. It was obvious this guy was hiding something.

Glen checked the husband's computer. It contained no personal emails. Who has a computer these days without an email account? Obviously, he deleted them. Glen confiscated the computers from Slater's home and office. At the police lab they were able to determine he had indeed erased all of his mail. They were still on the hard drive and the computer techs were able to retrieve them.

Glen spent the next few days reading through Slater's emails. He, too, had been emailing the opposite sex. To one woman in particular he described how unhappy he was in his marriage. When she asked him why he didn't file for divorce he told her it would be a big battle and he'd lose too much money. His wife brought in the lion's share of the family income.

In one email he wrote, "God willing, maybe she'll be killed in a car accident and I'll be free. I'd be better off if she were dead and I had her insurance money."

"Stupid bastard. Doesn't he know never to put it in writing," said Glen.

Now he had the information he needed to label the husband a prime suspect. He obtained a search warrant for the entire house. The crime scene investigators worked their way through the lower level.

"We've got blood!" yelled one of the men.

He had found a small spot on the door leading to the garage. It was at a height where it could easily have been one of the kids with a cut on his hand coming inside for a band-aid.   They collected a sample for DNA testing.

Glen walked through the house, his eyes scanning every inch of each room. When he walked into the master bedroom he felt the hair stand up on the back of his neck. He sensed negative energy in the room. His stomach twinged. Something definitely happened here.

His eyes swept the room, from one end to the other, for anything that didn't feel right to him—the bed. There were paintings on the wall where the head of the bed stood. The room was huge but the bed seemed to be off center to those paintings. He went back to the doorway to observe the position of the bed. He walked around it. In a house so meticulously decorated, a woman who took such care with interior design would not place a bed in such an odd location.

Glen dropped to his belly. He searched under the bed with his flashlight. Nothing. He tried to move the bed but stopped himself when he remembered of his arm.

"Hey, I need some help in here!" he called out.

Three men walked in.

"Move this bed across the room. I need to look under it."

The room had already been photographed so it took only moments for the men to flip the mattress and box spring against the wall. Before they moved the frame, Glen's keen eyes noticed the carpet. He stepped into the bed frame. Moving the mattress and box spring exposed two rectangular inserts cut into the carpet. Someone had repaired it, but why would the carpet under a bed need to be repaired? Armed with his pocketknife, he lifted one section of the patched carpet and set it aside. He then noticed the pad had also been replaced. He pried up the pad revealing what he was looking for. The bloodstain, in the wooden floor beneath the carpet, told the story. The blood sample from the wood matched the blood on the garage door. DNA taken from Christine's parents proved the blood was hers. But where was the body?

Chapter 4

"I'll schedule an appointment for next Thursday for Roxie's haircut," said Stacey. She scooted out of Becky's way so she could answer the phone.

Judy picked up her playful little Westie from the floor. The dog had discovered the clinic cat and was busy trying to get him to run, but the cat had seen far too many dogs over the years to be frightened by this rambunctious little white puppy.

Angie stepped out to the front desk to see who was next. The clinic normally closed thirty minutes earlier. The staff, exhausted from the busy week, didn't appreciate the late walk-ins who procrastinated until the last minute.

"Phone for you," said Becky as she helped Mrs. Wheelock with the two cats she planned to board over the weekend.

"This is Angie."

"Where are you? Nancy will be here tonight."

"Oh, sorry. It's been so busy here all week I forgot to tell you."

Clinical Death

"Tell me what?"

"I'm not coming into Sterling this week."

"Why? What happened to Taffy? She didn't get put to sleep did she?"

"No. We found a home for her."

"Okay, that's great, but next time call and let me know."

"I'm sorry. I will. I promise it won't happen again. Say hello to Nancy for me."

"Who was that?" asked Becky.

"Just a friend."

Angie called Mr. Dobson to follow her to the exam room. His black Labrador needed vaccinations. On the way down the hall Angie looked at her watch and moaned under her breath, "Why did he have to come in after hours for routine vaccinations? We should charge extra."

Becky and Stacey exchanged glances when two more clients walked in. One wanted dog food and the other asked if a vet could look at her horse with a gash in his chest. She had him in the horse trailer. The horse they could understand, but the after hours dog food was inexcusable, especially on a Friday night.

***

Dr. Allison Bradley said, "You guys go ahead and I'll lock up." The techs, from her Sterling, Colorado vet practice, were more than willing to oblige. They grabbed their keys and rushed out before someone showed up at the last minute.

Tina, one of the techs, said, "I still haven't figured out what gets into her about closing."

"What do you mean?" asked Robin.

"She's usually in a hurry to get out of the clinic herself. How many times has she left early and we've had to tell a client they had to come back in the morning because the vet had already left for the day. Then out of the blue she offers to close. It doesn't make any sense."

Robin thought about it, then replied, "Have you noticed it's always on Friday?"

"No, I hadn't thought of that. But you're right. I wonder if she's meeting someone here on Fridays?"

"Do you think she's having an affair?"

"Anything's possible. But I have better things to do than hang around here spying on her personal life," said Tina as she slammed the car door then waved good-bye.

Robin gazed at the clinic. Dr. Allison is a very attractive woman. I suppose it's possible she could be seeing someone, she thought. But when she's with her husband they always seem so happy.

An hour later there was a knock on the back door of the clinic. Dr. Bradley looked out the front window at the parking lot then went to unlock the door.

"Hi, Nancy. How was the drive?"

"Long. Do you have my two dogs?"

Clinical Death

"There's only going to be one this trip. The Newfoundland."

"What happened to the Corgi? I hope they didn't put her to sleep."

"No, she found a home."

"Great, that's good news. I have the perfect family back home in Wisconsin waiting for this dog," she said as Dr. Bradley handed her the leash.

"He's a pretty great dog. I think any family will love him."

"What's his story?"

"He had retained testicle. When the clients brought him in to have him neutered I explained the surgery would be a little more complicated and the cost would go up slightly since I had to go up into the body to find the testicle. They wanted me to leave it, but when I told them they were increasing the chances of cancer they told me to put him down instead."

"Why do people like that even own dogs?"

"They also have a female Newfoundland and, of course, they didn't spend the money to get her spayed so they ended up with fourteen puppies. They sold or gave away all but this guy. The kids wanted to keep him and the parents wised up enough to think about getting him neutered so he wouldn't breed back to his own mother. You know the rest."

Dr. Bradley helped Nancy load him into a crate in her Ford Freestyle.

"Who's this little guy?" asked Dr. Bradley.

"He's a she. I'm delivering her to Denver for a breeder from Michigan."

Dr. Bradley poked her fingers into the crate to let the Old English Sheepdog puppy slurp her fingers. The black and white ball of fluff with black eyes looked more like a stuffed animal than a real dog.

Nancy rearranged a few things in the car then prepared for the remainder of her journey into Denver.

Dr. Bradley waved as she drove off.

Nancy operated a dog transport business. She hauled them across the nation for breeders or buyers who didn't want to utilize the airlines to transport their dogs. She felt she could make the trip more comfortable for her furry passengers. She'd talk to them along the drive, stopping often to let them out of their crates for exercise. She checked into pet friendly motels and often let them sleep in bed with her. She adjusted her driving schedule to the stress level of the dog. Puppies tend to sleep many hours at a time enabling her to drive further between stops. Older dogs, especially those who weren't crate trained, were either allowed out of the crate to wander around the back of the car, occasionally slobbering on Nancy's neck while she drove, or she stopped more frequently to walk them.

Clinical Death

Nancy and her mother raised Golden Retrievers on their land in Paresh, Wisconsin. They had a small, but adequate facility. They kept it immaculately clean. When her mother tired of the show ring politics they closed the kennel. Occasionally, they boarded dogs for friends or family when they went on trips or vacations. Sometimes they would dog sit in the client's home. Exposure to the dog show world led Nancy to begin her transport business.

Glen stayed late at the office that night in Denver. The fact they couldn't find a murder weapon during the investigation bothered him. The situation is simplified when he knows the husband killed his wife and was foolish enough to wipe the blood off the weapon, leaving it in the house to be discovered.

He studied the report. According to the medical examiner, a left-handed individual with a blunt object struck Christine multiple times in the head. The search of the house found a number of baseball bats owned by the kids, but none of them showed traces of Christine's blood or skin.

When Glen asked the husband why he hadn't mentioned to anyone the bed had been moved, he told Glen he couldn't sleep in their bedroom without Christine. He'd been sleeping on the sofa. Glen noted that Frank skirted around the original question.

That comment didn't fly with Glen. If this guy and his wife were both contemplating divorce, it wouldn't bother him to sleep alone in his own bedroom. More often a spouse may have trouble sleeping in the room where he killed his wife. Glen suspected that was probably the case here.

Frank tried to convince Glen someone entered the family home, killed his wife, and cleaned up the area, including replacing the carpet, then left. Glen felt it must have been a spur of the moment reaction. Maybe Christine finally approached him about a divorce and he went ballistic. Had he taken any time to plan the murder, he surely could have been a bit more creative with his story. Nothing was missing from the house except Christine. There were no signs of breaking and entering. How would the perp know where in the basement to find matching carpet remnants and why bother? Why not just leave the body and walk away as quickly as possible? Obviously, the killer knew the family schedule and wasn't worried about someone walking in on him.

No way would Glen consider believing him, but he led Slater to believe so because he needed that body. He rubbed his tired eyes and looked at his watch. He remembered his new patient at home and the girls were probably wondering where their supper was.

Fortunately for Glen, working after hours allowed for less traffic on his commute from the city. Driving along the road, his headlights illuminated his neighbor's mailbox. He glanced through the darkness toward the

Clinical Death

house. That haunting feeling lingered with him about Ed's death.

When his headlights hit his own mailbox he realized it read... W A T K I N S. He made a mental note to run into town in the morning and check the hardware store for those gold and black stick-on letters and some paint to cover the previous owner's name.

He drove up the driveway and parked near the house. He sat in the pickup with the windows down listening to the sound of silence. He laid his head back against the headrest closing his eyes. He felt the throbbing in his head that began earlier in the evening but he struggled to ignore it.

He ran his hand through his hair to the back of his head, where the pounding intensified with each breath. With his jacket tossed over his shoulder he headed toward the house. He fed the dogs and turned them loose so they could run around the farm. While the girls were out exploring, he gave Taffy some one-on-one attention. He hoped to quickly build that special bond between dog and man.

He poured a glass of bourbon. It was late and he was too tired to cook. He made a sandwich and plopped down on the sofa to eat and listen to classic rock music. The dogs had returned to the house and all three of them eyed his sandwich just in case he decided he didn't really want it. He slid deeper into the sofa, placing one of the throw pillows over his eyes.

Cheyenne and Mieke barked a warning. Little Taffy hobbled along to the door behind them. Their barking caused Glen to sit up quickly. He must've dozed off. He blinked his eyes and called to the dogs. When he stood to look out the window he realized it was morning. He had spent the entire night on the sofa and the ache in his neck confirmed it.

He parted the curtain to see a female figure approaching the house carrying flowers and a picnic basket.

He checked to make sure he was still dressed as he remained in a sleepy fog then opened the door.

"Jennifer! Holy Shit, what're you doing here?"

"I'm sorry, Glen. Did I wake you?"

"No. I mean, yes. I mean, the dogs barked. What time is it?"

"Nine-thirty."

Glen snapped into alertness. "No way." He checked his watch in disbelief.

"Come in, come in."

"Thank you. What a lovely drive to your new residence, Detective Karst."

He had reminded her many times to call him Glen. She did on occasion, but preferred his title as a salutation.

Clinical Death

He wondered if it was a method she used to keep a professional relationship between them.

"Here, these are for you. I know men never seem to buy themselves flowers, but it does cheer up a home nicely. Don't you agree?"

"Thanks," said Glen. "How did you know where I lived? I mean, how did you get directions?" Glen thought about what he said. "I guess that's a pretty stupid thing to say under the circumstances."

"Not really, even psychics stop for directions. The gentleman at the Wallace Post Office was kind enough to direct me to the proper roads to arrive at your farm. I thought breakfast would be appropriate to bring along. Not having dined with you for breakfast I was not quite sure what you preferred. I assumed you had coffee so I bought a nice cinnamon coffeecake and fruit."

"No, that's perfect. Come into the kitchen and I'll make us some coffee."

"I really did not mean to intrude. You probably wanted to sleep in on your morning off."

"No. That was never my intention. I worked late last night then fell asleep on the sofa. It's so quiet here I just kept sleeping. Could you excuse me for one minute?"

Glen slipped off to the bathroom to brush his hair and teeth. He grabbed a clean shirt from the closet. He joined Jennifer with his shirttails hanging out as he buttoned up. He remained comfortably barefoot.

69

Patricia A. Bremmer

"Do you mind if I look around a bit?" she asked.

"Be my guest." Glen kept an immaculately clean house, car and desk at his office. Some of his colleagues thought he had an OC disorder. He explained he's neither obsessive nor compulsive but liked things neat and tidy. Work was stressful enough without having to deal with disturbing clutter.

Jennifer strolled from room to room admiring the old farmhouse. She sensed many happy times with lots of love and laughter from the family who lived there in the past.

Glen set out two cups of coffee and two slices of cake. He had forgotten to buy napkins but improvised with paper towels. He went off to join Jennifer. He found her in the spare bedroom gazing out the window. The sunlight shone through the glass across her face. Somehow she looked different to him this morning. He realized most of his time spent with Jennifer she was in a suit of some sort, whether it be a skirt or slacks—always the perfect lady. Jennifer had dark auburn hair that she wore cropped short and tidy. That was it, he thought.

Jennifer's hair fell softly down her back nearly to her waist. She wore the front the same as usual with her bangs brushed softly over to one side. He didn't notice it at first. She had barrettes above her ears guiding the long hair away from her face.

70

Clinical Death

Blue jeans, he thought. Jennifer not only has her hair down but she's wearing blue jeans and tennis shoes. He noticed her figure for the first time—slender with a tiny waist and full breasts. For years he thought of her as the psychic professional woman. He never considered her in the way men look at women.

"Is there something wrong?" she asked.

Glen realized he'd been staring.

"Uh, breakfast is ready."

Jennifer grinned, "I do look different from what you're accustomed to, don't I?"

"Are you doing your mind reading stuff with me?" he teased.

"No, your face."

"I had no idea your hair was so long. It's beautiful."

"Thank you. I love long hair but in my business I have such a difficult time gaining the respect of others I wear it short. That's why you've probably not seen me without my wig."

"You wear a wig? I would never have guessed. I suppose I don't really know anyone who wears one— maybe a couple of guys with really bad rugs. Yours looks so natural. I guess I'm just surprised."

"It should look natural. It's made from my own hair. With hair this long you don't miss the five or six inches it takes to create a short-haired wig."

"Well, you look nice."

Jennifer tugged at her blouse, "I assumed blue jeans and tennis shoes would be a more appropriate attire when one visits in the country. I was unsure if you would have me help slop the hogs or whatever one does with them."

"No hogs yet," replied Glen as he guided her to the kitchen.

She sipped coffee and continued to admire the grounds out the window. She ran her hand along the table and back of the chairs.

"You did a magnificent job constructing these."

"How did you know I built them?"

She took Glen's hand gently placing it on the top of the table.

"Close your eyes. Relax. Can you feel the vibration of the wood? Can you feel the energy? Imagine all of the atoms and molecules dancing beneath your hand. Now, can you remember how you felt as you worked the wood? Your energy mixed with the energy of the wood. You and the table share energy. The moment I touched it I felt your energy. The intensity told me you had done more than owned it and cleaned it, you constructed it with a part of you left behind."

Glen noticed the longer he left his hand on the table the warmer it became. He thought he felt the tingling sensation Jennifer spoke of but then he wondered

Clinical Death

if he had only wanted to feel it. Somehow, she had to know he was the carpenter. Once again he had to credit her abilities.

"So what brings you out my way this morning?" he asked.

"Curiosity. I've not spent any time on a real farm."

"This isn't exactly a real farm. It could be I suppose, but since I have no livestock I consider it nothing more than a house in the country. I do plan to get a few horses once I'm settled in. Who knows, maybe even a steer or two to fatten for the freezer."

"You could do that? Eat something you raised?"

"Jennifer, I was brought up on a farm. We ate everything we grew. Actually, my parents lived in this very county until their house was destroyed by a tornado. They were ready to retire anyway so they sold the land and the buildings and moved to Arizona."

"Could we take a stroll outdoors?" she asked.

"Absolutely, let me get my boots on."

Jennifer stepped out onto the porch to wait.

Glen called to the dogs and they were off on their stroll, as Jennifer put it. As they walked along, Glen talked. He explained his life growing up as a country boy. She marveled at his stories and would not have guessed his background had he not shared it with her. Glen seemed to think Jennifer read his mind and knew his every thought. She could only hone in on him when she had a question or concern. She preferred to live her life as normally as anyone else. Having learned to turn off her psychic abilities at will, she only used them when she worked or wrote.

"Can you tell me what is being planted? I watched the tractors in the fields on my way here."

"Sure, let's take a drive and I can explain it to you a little better."

As they drove past the Kurtleman place, Jennifer took Glen's arm.

"Stop here, please," she said.

Glen knew Jennifer sensed the same thing he did. Some intense energy drew her attention. He remained silent as he pulled over to the side of the road.

"Who lives here?" she asked.

"No one," he replied.

"Glen, the energy here is strong. If someone lived here I'd have to say they were in danger. Are you sure no one lives here?"

"No, Jennifer, no one lives here but someone recently died here."

"May we go onto the property?"

"Of course, the new owner lives out of state."

Glen put his pickup in reverse then realigned the tires and drove forward into the driveway. He parked near the house instead of by the shop where Ed's body had

Clinical Death

been found. He climbed out of the pickup, running around to Jennifer's door to let her out.

"What a sad place," she remarked. "A very, very sad place. An unhappy man lived here. He had a drinking problem. I believe he tried to, how would you put it, drown his sorrows with alcohol."

Although Glen believed in Jennifer's talents, he still caught himself withholding information as a sort of test. He continually needed to be convinced. He followed her as she wandered around, touching the house and fence in front. She smelled the lilac blooms.

"Your dog," she said. "Your little dog."

She turned quickly to Glen.

"Your little dog used to live here."

"That would be Taffy and, yes, she used to live here."

"Her owner, the man with the drinking problem. He died here."

Glen watched her work. Even though she spoke to him with a questioning tone to her voice, he knew she was not expecting a response, but rather questioning out loud as she tried to piece the story together.
Soon Jennifer's pace quickened as they approached the shop building. She stopped short, turning in a complete circle as her eyes rested on the ground.

"He died here, where I'm standing."

"That's right. This is where they found his body. His pickup accidentally rolled onto him while he was checking something underneath it."

"No, Glen. That's not correct. Didn't anyone mention his body was face down when they found him? If he had been working beneath the truck, would he not have been lying on his back so he could look up at whatever concerned him?"

"Are you sure?"

"Yes, I'm absolutely certain."

"What else can you tell me?"

"He was not alone when he died."

"Someone else was here when the truck rolled over on him and left him here to die?"

"Was his truck white?"

"Yes."

"I see someone behind the wheel of a white truck. At the same time, I see this man, Ed was his name, correct?"

"Yes, his name was Ed."

"I see someone in behind the wheel and Ed under the tire."

"Jennifer, if what you see is accurate then this was no accident."

"No, Glen it was no accident. It was very much planned. I'm sure this is not coming as a surprise to you."

Clinical Death

"I had a feeling something wasn't what it seemed. I couldn't quite get a grasp on it. I stopped by here shortly after they found the body. I noticed the flat ground beneath the tires and questioned how the truck could possibly have rolled onto him."

"Did you check to see if the key was in the off position? Our mystery person turned off the engine before leaving."

"No, I wasn't on the case. I missed out on the crime scene. By the time I got here the neighbors had already been here. The ground showed multiple footprints. I had bad vibes but nothing to go on. Can you tell me what the driver looked like?"

"I'm sorry, Glen. I can't even tell you if it was a man or a woman."

Glen ran his hand through his hair in frustration. He knew what was coming. Right next door to his new home a homicide happened without any hint of an investigation. What kind of trouble would he stir up bringing this to the attention of the local sheriff's department? Cal told him there hadn't been a murder in this county in over one hundred years—so much for relaxing at his new country home.

Chapter 5

Glen sifted through mounds of paperwork on his desk. He tried desperately to direct his focus to the current case.

Finding the blood and repaired carpet left no doubt in his mind Christine met with a fatal attack in her own bedroom. Without a body the charges would be difficult to make stick. If Slater's attorney presented the case properly to the jury, he could create a reasonable doubt.

Christine planned to leave him and there were other men involved in her life. The husband's theory of someone coming into their home and killing Christine could hold up in court. Glen thought tampering with the crime scene in an attempt to cover up, leaned more toward the husband than an intruder unless, of course, the bad guy wanted to frame the husband. Prove what isn't to prove what is, he thought.

A confession without a body and a weapon seemed highly unlikely. Glen needed proof. No matter how hard he tried to maintain his focus the homicide that happened

Clinical Death

in his own backyard crept in. How could he not believe Jennifer Parker? Her abilities as a psychic helping with crimes were nothing less than remarkable. Having worked with her over the years, he learned she maintained an air of modesty. She did not expect praise or a pat on the back for her work. She did not wish to awe the people she worked with and would be the first to admit when she was unsure of an event, person or place. Yet, she was so confident about the circumstances surrounding the death of his neighbor.

Glen slid his chair away from the desk in frustration. He went to the office coffee pot to pour a cup, only to find the last few drops burning in the bottom. He marveled at how some of the men in the office were so damned helpless when it came to a simple domestic task.

He carried the pot to the lounge area where he washed the burned flavor from the stained glass. He filled it with fresh water then returned to the coffee maker to start a fresh pot. He leaned his back to the counter that held the coffee equipment. He observed the office as it buzzed with the daily work of phone calls, discussions among detectives, computers keys tapping away and the sound of shuffling papers. Was he really ready to return to all of this?

He filled his cup then started back to his desk. He followed the urge to turn back to the coffeemaker and saw a line of fellow workers filling their cups. It was obvious to him who the lazy ones were when it came to making coffee as they kept one eye on the coffee counter waiting for someone else to make it. He shook his head then returned to his desk.

Bill stopped by his desk seeking something to eat.

"What do you want?" asked Glen, already knowing the answer. He noticed the shadow of the stain on Bill's shirt and tie from the jelly donut that dripped days ago.

"Just thought you might have some donuts or something to eat."

"This ain't a cafeteria, Buddy. Ever thought about buying your own?"

"I suppose I could. Hell, maybe I could even spring for a few dozen donuts for the whole office."

At first Glen thought a light turned on in Bill's head and he might show up with food to share, but he quickly decided that would never happen.

Bill sat on the edge of Glen's desk crinkling his papers.

"Hey, get your fat ass of off my desk. Use the chair."

"What's bugging you? No leads on that missing body I take it?"

"Nothing."

"What about the weapon?"

"Nadda."

Clinical Death

"Something else is bugging you. Spill it. Is it Debbie?"

"No, it's not Debbie."

Glen sat back in his chair, his elbow on one armrest. He leaned forward while stroking his chin with his hand. Bill, although nothing like Glen, was a good cop with great instincts. Glen gnawed the inside of his lip. He knew Bill disliked Jennifer and all that she stood for. Maybe telling him what he thought had happened to his neighbor, followed by Jennifer's comments, might give him an inkling of what to expect if he went to the Wallace sheriff's department with his suspicions.

"My neighbor was found dead and the local law enforcement ruled it an accident. But I smell a homicide."

Curious now, Bill asked, "What makes you think homicide? I thought the town you moved to was a sleepy little burg."

"It is, or at least I think it is. I heard about it after the fact. I stopped by the scene to look around. This guy's pickup rolled over the top of him."

"Yeah, well Glen, that does happen."

"On flat ground?"

"Was it in gear?"

"I don't know."

"Was it running?"

"I don't know."

"So you're basing a homicide on the fact that the ground was flat?"

"I had a gut feeling and Jennifer Parker confirmed it."

Bill rolled his eyes. "Don't tell me that old dame has you believing you're some kind of damned psychic like her?"

"She's no older than you, my friend. I think she's about fifty."

"Don't change the god damned subject on me. You're one hell of a good cop. Don't let her ruin your abilities as a topnotch detective. Don't go believing in all of this voodoo stuff. She's a crackpot."

"How do you explain the help she's been on some of our cases?"

"She's a lucky crackpot. I don't know. Just, keep her away from me."

"Don't you even want to hear what she had to say?"

"Okay, let's have it. One of these times we're gonna be able to prove her a fake."

Glen wondered now whether telling Bill was a good idea or not, but it did help him decide not to share Jennifer's comments with the Wallace sheriff's department.

"Jennifer told me the guy drove a white pickup, even though the pickup was no longer there."

Clinical Death

"And how many farmers drive white pickups? Lots. Her odds were good."

"Do you want me to go on or not?"

"Sure, sure. Go on."

"She said he was found lying face down with the front tire crushing him. She also said he wasn't alone when he died. She said someone was behind the wheel of the pickup and turned the engine off before they left."

"And you believed her?"

"Don't you think it strange if he was checking something under the pickup he'd be face down?"

Bill's facial expression took on a more serious look. He had to agree with Jennifer's statement. His mind worked quickly to envision the scene while trying to come up with a way to discredit her.

"And you checked with the sheriff's department to verify the body position from the photos taken at the scene?"

"Not yet. I wasn't quite sure how to approach them. I'm out of my jurisdiction there and they're happy thinking their county doesn't have homicides. When I talked to the old vet, Cal, buddy I've known since I was a kid, he told me not to stir up trouble."

"Have you thought about taking his advice?"

"Sure, but could you, if you felt there was a homicide gone undetected, especially right next door?"

"Maybe you should just leave it to the locals and focus more on this," he pointed to Glen's stack of folders.

Glen looked at the folders then at Bill as he walked away. When he felt this strongly about a case, he knew he couldn't let it rest.

He pored over the emails removed from Frank's computer to the women he'd been corresponding with. He obviously tried to impress them with his wide range of interests, neglecting to disclose he was married with four kids.

Glen's intense anger toward men who abused women or children remained the driving force to see this through and make sure Frank was put behind bars. He desperately wanted to find Christine's body so she could be laid to rest, giving closure to her parents. Their faces and tears tugged at Glen's heart each time he spoke with them or called to inform them of the lack of new evidence.

He placed the emails in separate piles for each woman Frank romanced online. "The bastard uses the same lines on all of these women."

When he'd finished sorting the emails one stack rose above the others. He had been emailing this woman multiple times per day for months. Glen decided to start there.

He found all the usual garbage married men write to other women, how his wife doesn't understand him, how hard he works and she doesn't appreciate it. He embellished how great and athletic he was. He bragged about everything from playing basketball with his buddies on Wednesday nights to his near perfect bowling scores and his outstanding ability on the golf course.

"Golf course?" whispered Glen. He read through the officer's reports again and the "return and inventory" produced from the search of the home. The kids' baseball bats were listed, but no mention of golf clubs. They were looking for a blunt object that created the blood spatter pattern they found on the walls. Frank cleaned the walls removing most but not all, of the blood. The trained eye of the crime scene investigator was much more keen than the average citizen, especially a frenzied citizen.

Glen's mind raced through the rooms of the house in question. He thought of the garage, the basement, the storage shed out back. If Frank was a golfer, where did he keep his clubs—at the clubhouse, perhaps? He looked at his watch. It was too late in the day to pursue another search warrant.

Glen played in the backyard with his dogs. Little Taffy wanted to join in, but her leg in a cast made that difficult. He let the dogs into the kitchen while he prepared their bowls. When Mieke stood up, wagging her tail to follow Glen to her side of the kitchen where he fed her, he noticed blood on the kitchen floor. He placed all three bowls along different walls so he could prevent the dogs from eating each other's supper. He checked Mieke for signs of heat. Sure enough, she was in her heat cycle but, unfortunately, he didn't know if this was the first day or not. He questioned the timing of having puppies when they just moved into the house. He picked up the phone to call Janet.

"Dr. Jensen."

"Janet. Glen. Mieke's in heat. What'd ya think? Should we do it or skip this cycle?"

"If you want my opinion, I'd much rather be dealing with a litter of puppies during the summer than the winter months. There'd be a lot less mess. They could go outdoors when they're pups instead of keeping them indoors under heat lamps."

"I guess you're right. Where do we go from here?"

"Do you work tomorrow?"

"I'm not scheduled to, but had planned to anyway. I'm working on a case that...never mind. Why?"

"If you want to bring her in tomorrow we can draw some blood to get a baseline for a blood serum progesterone test and while she's there we'll do a vaginal swab to look for the number of parabasal cells and see if there's any cornification yet."

"Any special time?"

"We open at eight. Can you be there about seven forty-five so we don't cut into some other client's appointment?"

"We'll be there."

Clinical Death

When Glen arrived at the clinic the next morning the front doors were still locked. He walked Mieke around to the back. He noticed Angie leaving out the back door carrying the limp body of a dog.

"Hey, Ang."

She jumped. "Jesus Glen, you scared the shit out of me. I thought I was alone."

"What's up with the dog?"

He lifted the head of the blue merle Australian Shepherd.

Angie backed away from Glen. "The owners didn't want her, they're moving away. They brought her in here to be put to sleep. I'm just disposing of her body."

Glen ran his fingers through the thick coat of the dog.

Once again, Angie backed away. "I'd better get going. She's pretty heavy."

"Great markings on her face. Too bad," said Glen with a heavy heart. He looked down at Mieke sitting obediently at his side, wondering what her fate would have been had he not adopted her.

He walked in through the back door to find Janet. They bumped into each other in the hall.

"Oh good, you're here. I have an emergency surgery getting prepped, let's get this blood drawn."

Glen followed her to the exam room where he lifted Mieke to the table.

"Angie," called Janet.

"She's out back," said Glen.

"What's she doing out back?"

"Disposing of that Australian Shepherd you put down this morning."

"What? That's odd. We put them in a storage room until evening then we dispose of the bodies...well, never mind. I swear, that girl has a mind of her own sometimes."

Susie walked past the room.

"Susie, let's get a blood draw and a swab on this dog."

Susie handed Janet a syringe while Glen held Mieke. She reached to take his place and he said, "No, that's okay, I've got her. Needles don't bother me and she expects me to stay with her."

She gathered the cotton swab and a glass slide for the vaginal smear. While Glen held the dog, Janet drew the blood and Susie swabbed the vagina.

"I've gotta go. Susie, run a progesterone test and have Cal look at that slide." She darted out of the room.

Glen put Mieke back in the truck. He watched as Susie ran the test. Angie walked past the door.

"Hey, Angie, go find Cal to come look at this slide after I stain it," said Susie.

Moments later Cal arrived in the lab.

"Glen, what're you doing here so early?"

Clinical Death

"My shepherd's in heat."

Susie was not quite finished with the three-step process for staining the slide.

Cal waited.

"How's the house coming along?"

"Pretty good, I don't have much time for it now that I'm back at work."

Glen really wanted to ask more questions about Ed Kurtleman but didn't know how to broach the subject.

"So did Ed's brother get all of his cattle sold?"

"Yeah, but he didn't get a good price for them. Ed didn't do such a great job with them. Most of them should have been culled years ago. These last few years with the bottle really took their toll on Ed. I guess, come to think of it, he lost his life to booze."

"The tests are ready," said Susie.

Glen let the subject of Ed drop. He'd pick it up with Sheriff Tate.

"You've got a ways to go, she's barely in heat. Look here at the color of the sample from your dog and the two control samples. See how dark pink the fluid is in her vial. That matches the dark pink negative vial. What we're striving for is this pale, almost straw-colored pink. That means she's had her LH surge."

"And that means?" asked Glen.

"That would be her luteinizing hormone that triggers her body to release the eggs. Once the eggs are released, with dogs, you have to wait a few days for them to sort of thin out or ripen before a sperm cell can penetrate."

"What's this other test for?"

"This is a little more old-fashioned. We can tell post ovulation rather than predict upcoming ovulation. Here, look here. See those big plump cells that look like fried eggs with big yolks?"

"Yeah."

"Well, those are called parabasal cells. When she's closer or has ovulated, those will turn a little more square at the corners and the nucleus will shrink. Kinda looks like it folds over on itself. When you bring her in again I'll show ya."

"How often do I have to bring her in?"

"Every other day until you breed her. Do you have a stud lined up?"

"No, not yet."

"If you can't find any locally or in Denver, you can always use shipped frozen semen."

"I'll visit with some of the guys in the canine unit and get back to you on that one."

"See ya in two days then. I've got work to do."

As Glen drove away from the clinic he noticed the police station in downtown Wallace. It seemed as though his subconscious mind controlled his pickup as he found

Clinical Death

himself turning into the parking lot at the side of the building.

Inside, he asked to speak to Sheriff Tate.

A tall, dark-haired man with a thick mustache dressed in a brown sheriff's uniform stepped into the room. He extended his hand.

"I'm Scott Tate, how can I help you?"

"Hi, I'm Glen Karst from the Denver PD. I bought the old Watkins place south of town."

"Nice to meet you. Is there a problem?"

Glen noticed everyone in the office had their eyes upon them.

"Is there somewhere we could talk?"

Scott took Glen into his office and closed the door.

"Now, what can I do for you? Are you here in an official capacity?"

"No, well, not really. I was wondering if you'd share some information with me about my neighbor, Ed Kurtleman."

"Why, did you know Ed?"

"No, but since we were neighbors, I hoped I could learn a little more about him and his death."

"Not much to tell. Ed lived alone. He drank too much and it got the best of him."

"Was an autopsy performed?"

"Yes, he was loaded and the cause of death was the weight of the truck crushing his body."

"Were you curious why the truck rolled on flat ground?"

"He probably had it in gear when he climbed out to check something. Hell, he probably passed out and fell under the front tire."

Glen thought for a minute. That would explain why he was face down. He could've been checking a tire and fell over.

"Would you mind if I looked at the photos from the scene?"

Tate studied Glen's face while expressing annoyance on his own.

He stood up and went to the file cabinet, opening the second drawer. He thumbed through the files, finding it then tossing it on the desk.

"Kind of a big burly guy, wasn't he?" said Glen as he studied the photos. He read through the report.

"Says here the truck was an automatic. He had it in park and the ignition was in the off position. What do you suppose caused that truck to roll forward onto him when it was on flat ground?"

He walked behind Glen to study the photo over his shoulder. Glen flipped to the toxicology portion of the autopsy. Not only was the blood alcohol level at 2.0, but also tests showed Ace Promazine mixed with Xylazine in his bloodstream.

Clinical Death

"What are these drugs? I'm not familiar with them," asked Glen.

"That's a tranquilizer blend for cattle and horses."

"What's it doing in Ed?"

"He probably injected himself with it."

"Why?"

"Hell, Detective Karst."

"Call me Glen."

"Okay, Glen. Ed was a drunk who owned livestock. Do you know how many sober farmers and ranchers have livestock meds floating in their bloodstreams? Ask any of them. You're about to inject an animal and it jumps and you stick yourself. Happens all the time. My guess is, Ed was trying to care for one of his animals when he was too drunk to walk and stuck himself.

"Did you notice his pickup? Ed's run that thing into just about everything on his farm. Look how beat up it is. He's even run over his own dog a bunch of times. I wonder where his dog is? I didn't see her around the day we found Ed."

"I have her. She was at the clinic. Ed ran over her again. They were gonna have to put her down, so I took her."

Scott softened his attitude toward the big city detective who was sticking his nose where it didn't belong. Glen always wondered why they were so defensive—the small town cops. To Glen they were all brothers...looking after each other, sharing information and solving crimes.

"Is there something bothering you about this case?" he asked.

"Have you ever considered the possibility of a homicide?"

"Homicide? Here in Wallace? Not hardly. Look, just because Ed's pickup rolled over on him doesn't indicate homicide. We have no motive and no one had anything to gain except his brother. He ended up with a bunch of old cows and a rundown farm. Ed may have been a drunk, but he had no enemies that I know of."

That part had Glen puzzled—no motive, but sometimes motive is more elusive than evidence.

"Look, Glen, we treat every death as a homicide until we prove otherwise. Ed had been out drinking 'til he closed the bar. I have a number of witnesses to attest to that. We saw nothing at the scene to show he'd been robbed or any signs of vandalism. He still had his wallet with three hundred dollars in it. I think you're trying to make something out of nothing."

"It's not what it seems," said Glen.

"And just how do you know that?"

"My gut."

"Sometimes what you feel in your gut might not be what I feel in mine," said Scott.

Clinical Death

"My gut has been right so many times that I've learned to rely heavily on it. "

"And it told you Ed had been murdered?"

"I just question whether Ed was alone when he died. Someone else could have been behind the wheel of the pickup."

Tate had no desire to listen to any further comments Glen had to share. He returned to the paperwork on his desk.

"Well, Detective Karst, I'm a busy man. I have crimes to solve. Why don't you keep your gut instinct in Denver where it belongs and we'll handle the deaths and crime in our county. If we need your services, we know where to find you."

Chapter 6

Glen spent most of the morning phoning country clubs to inquire about Frank Slater's membership. No luck.

Next he called public golf courses to check their membership rosters. He located one near Slater's residence. He drove over to visit with the employees. Glen preferred face-to-face conversations whenever possible. One of his strong points was his ability to read people. An amateur criminal had difficulty hiding guilt, as did the pros, if he played them correctly.

Glen liked to toy with the person he's interviewing. He might take the friendly approach to gain his confidence by giving him someone to confide in. Many need to speak about the incident to someone and Glen's soft voice and sincere attitude encouraged many a criminal to spill the story in great detail before remembering he was speaking to the police.

Other times he might take on the role of a less than intelligent detective, allowing the perp to let his guard down, feeling confident that Glen has no way of figuring out the case. How shocked they are when they finally become aware that they've been conned by a keen mind.

One by one, Glen visited with the employees at the golf course. He learned Frank only golfed on occasion and had never registered for any of the tournaments held at that course. He always golfed alone and no one had ever met his wife. She was not on the membership roster.

They checked further records to see if Slater stored a golf cart or if he kept his clubs on the premises. The answer to both questions was no.

Glen sat in his car staring out over the lush fairways, frustrated as hell because he knew Slater killed his wife. Glen was convinced of Slater's guilt and he knew Frank understood that but there wasn't a damn thing he could do about it without a body or a weapon. Christine's car was still missing as well.

Slater remained firm with his story about an intruder entering their home, killing his wife, covering the scene and leaving with the body—probably in Christine's car.

Christine's car, he thought. He picked up the file from the seat next to him. The investigation centered on finding Christine's car, a red 2005 Toyota Camry. What about Frank's car? During the course of the investigation, was his car searched thoroughly? Yes. The report stated no blood, signs of a struggle or evidence were found in Frank's car. So immediately the focus turned to her car. According to the report, he had no golf clubs on the list of contents from his car. He wanted Frank's car to be swept more thoroughly.

He needed more evidence to get this guy into a courtroom. When Glen knows, without a shadow of a doubt, someone is guilty he can't let it rest. Too many guilty persons are released for lack of sufficient evidence. When the big case loads pile up on desks, many other detectives would toss in the towel and move on, but not Detective Karst. Maybe that's why his forty-hour-a-week job takes him over one hundred hours, maybe that's why he solves more cases, maybe that's why his wife walked out on their marriage. Being a detective is not merely a job to him, it's become his way of life. Cases run through his mind until he drowns them out with bourbon. Maybe he is obsessed as some of his cronies suggest, however, his obsession is not about how clean he keeps his surroundings but rather how clean he tries to keep the streets.

On his way home he drove into Ed's farmyard again. He parked his pickup and sat there waiting for something to come to him. He often wished Jennifer Parker's comments about his own untapped abilities waiting to burst forward would do just that; he was so ready for that breakthrough. That extra something to push him one step closer to solving every crime that crossed his desk. He closed his eyes with wishful anticipation, but nothing. He heard his dogs barking. They knew the sound of his pickup as it neared home. They probably wondered what happened to him. He started the engine and drove slowly to the farm.

The next morning he repeated his earlier visit to the vet clinic. The two tests were run again, but no significant change. He knew he had better choose a stud dog soon, but his mind was stuck on the two cases. He went to the front desk to schedule another appointment.

Rosemary Boyle held her little Schnauzer, Libby.

"I need to get her hair cut while she's here, but wait until a few days before I return. That way it'll still be fresh when I take her home. I just love the way she smells when she gets her hair cut," she said.

Becky smiled at Karst as she wrote down Rosemary's request.

"How long will Libby be staying with us?" asked Becky.

"Two weeks. No, make that two weeks and one day from today. We're going to London to see our daughter. She goes to school there, did you know that?"

"No, ma'am, I sure didn't. How exciting. Have you been there before?"

"Once, but that was a bad memory."

"I'm sorry. Did you have a bad time?"

"No. Being with my daughter was wonderful, but poor Libby here had a bad time. Louis booted her out of the house and put her in the barn. He locked her in a stall with food and water and never checked on her. She spilled her water, probably the first day. She went eight days being locked up. By the time I got home she was nearly dead. Thank God Cal came in after hours and started an I.V. on her. We weren't sure she was going to make it. Cal said he wasn't sure if her kidneys would shut down.

"I'm not taking any chances this time. I'm boarding her here where I know she'll be safe."

"Isn't Louis going with you?"

"Who knows? We have tickets for both of us to leave tomorrow, but he's so darn stubborn. He's worried about getting his corn planted. I don't see what two weeks will hurt. Besides, there's rain in the forecast so he probably can't get into the field anyway."

Rosemary turned to see Glen standing behind her. She couldn't help but notice how handsome he was.

"Excuse me. I didn't realize someone was waiting and here I've just been rambling on and on about my worthless husband. I'm so sorry. My, that's a beautiful dog."

"Thanks, I like her. Don't mind me. Go ahead and finish your business with the lovely Becky."

Becky blushed a bright crimson.

Clinical Death

Glen knew she would, but he thought if she became accustomed to his teasing she could learn to relax around him. After all, he was just another client.

Soon Becky finished with Rosemary and handed Glen his new appointment card. He loaded Mieke and drove home.

He had the remainder of the day scheduled off from the office but not from his duty as a cop. He volunteered to teach a woman's self-defense class. With his attitude about crime against women, he thought it was the least he could do to teach those who are interested how to defend themselves both mentally and tactically.

Whenever he could, he found other cops to volunteer for his class. What previously was a two-day class he condensed into one day. He begins each class by having a lecture/discussion session that takes up the first two hours. During the presentation he explains to the women the psychology of the attacker and the victim. Being more cautious about where and when you go out, along with confident body language, can prevent many attacks. One phrase he uses with each class is, "Don't present yourself as a victim and then don't become one."

He goes into detail about what one can and cannot physically do to prevent being attacked. He explains what procedures to follow after an assault. He stresses you should do what needs to be done to keep yourself alive.

The remainder of the class is six hours of physical training. He teaches the women how to break free from the assailant depending upon the approach. Women tend to not want to harm other women in the class, but don't seem to mind bringing a volunteer police officer to his knees or onto the ground. Actually, it gives them more of a sense of empowerment. Glen enforces the need to think clearly and to react out of knowledge, not fear. Once a woman takes control of the situation, many times the assailant will flee when realizing the victim fails to be the easy target he hoped for.

Today, as he worked with the room full of women and volunteer officers, he kept his mind on Christine. He wondered if she would be alive today had she been trained in the art of self-defense. If she had a bit of training in the Russian martial arts could she have turned away her attacker?

His thoughts about Christine interfered with his focus. She worked the day before her disappearance. The kids were away at a church sponsored slumber party. Frank said she left for work like she always did in the morning. That meant they were alone in the house all night. He told Glen they were together for the entire time. He left for work after she did. Without a body there is no way to determine the time of death. Could she have returned home as Frank suggested? Could there have really been an intruder or a lover's rendezvous at the house?

He already questioned the neighbors, friends, family and co-workers. He talked with the men she emailed and the women Frank emailed. How could a first-time killer be so lucky to have such an airtight case?

He pondered the intruder scenario. There was no sign of forced entry, no fingerprints were found anywhere in the house except those of family members. His story would have been more plausible had he not tried to cover the crime by changing the carpet. An intruder or lover wouldn't have taken the time.

Glen brought his mind back to the class. He asked if anyone had any further questions. It appeared the women were exhausted both physically as well as mentally. He always overloaded them with information. Each time he closed the class he noticed how the facial expressions of the women had changed. The meek, giggling, nervous women who walked in the door transformed into the calm, more self-assured look they now possessed. No one ever complained and they always wanted additional classes.

At the beginning of class the women were nearly silent, whispering to only the friend they may have come with. Then, as fate would have it, Glen overheard two women talking.

"I'm so glad I decided to take this class. I've been on edge since that Slater woman disappeared. When I saw her face on the news and they said foul play was suspected I felt chills. I registered her for her room the night before her disappearance."

"No kidding. I wonder why she checked into a motel when she has a house in Cherry Creek."

"That's what I wondered. Then I thought maybe she had a boyfriend or a fight with her husband. I learned a long time ago to mind my own business. I remember the time my doctor checked in with a lady friend. Boy, was that embarrassing for both of us."

Glen waited until most of the students had left the area. He kept his eye on the woman who spoke of Christine Slater. He walked over to the two friends.

"May I have a word with you?" he asked.

She smiled at her friend. When she first entered the room she was instantly attracted to Glen and now she hoped he was about to ask her for her phone number.

"Sure."

Her friend walked away to give them some private time.

"I didn't mean to eavesdrop but I overheard you talking about the Christine Slater case and I'd like to ask you a few questions."

Disappointed he had a professional reason for speaking to her, she answered, "Sure."

Clinical Death

"First of all, what motel do you work for?"

"I work for the Ramada Inn."

Glen pulled his notebook from his back pocket.

"I'm sorry Michelle, I don't remember your last name."

"Helm."

"Great, thanks. Now you say Ms. Slater checked into a room the night before her disappearance?"

"Yes."

"Are you absolutely sure?"

"Absolutely. I remember wondering why and I studied her face a long time, trying to figure out the answer. She didn't appear nervous like some of our guests who are having an affair. I couldn't guess."

"Did she use her correct name and address when she checked in?"

"I can tell you yes on that one, too. When I saw her face on television I was at work. I went back to the computer to check it out. It was her, alright."

Glen finally had a break in the case. Fate has a strange way of helping out when all else fails. He was pleased with himself for his habit of constantly having his ears and eyes open in all situations. Evidence can surface when you least expect it. Now he could prove that Frank Slater lied about spending the night with his wife.

He began to piece a scenario together. Obviously, they must've had a fight. She left the house alive and checked into a motel. He must have waited for her to return, then killed her. He probably hid her body until he could dispose of her properly. He had to work fast to kill her, hide the body and clean up his mess.

Glen needed to go back to Slater's place of employment to be sure he was actually at work the entire time he said he was.

Unfortunately, it was after hours and would be closed until morning.

He went back home and went over the files once again. There had to be something he missed. He poured a glass of bourbon then stepped out onto the porch to enjoy the night air. His dogs raced around the farmyard sniffing everywhere. How much can the smells change from one day to the next he wondered? Then he thought he was not totally unlike the dogs, sniffing through the Slater file over and over hoping to find something new.

He knew the prosecuting attorney had a weak case. The defense attorney had no proof there was a visitor or intruder, only Slater's theory. Reasonable doubt could still be the problem. All he had to do was create a reasonable doubt with the jury and Slater would walk. He still needed that damned body and murder weapon because juries consistently conjure up their own reasonable doubt to avoid being responsible, even with strong cases, for presenting a guilty verdict.

Clinical Death

Glen sipped his bourbon, emptying his glass then went back inside for a refill. When he returned to the swing he watched Cheyenne stop and prick her ears. Mieke soon followed her lead, as did little Taffy, looking in the direction of Ed's place. Glen turned his head in the same direction.

He thought he heard the distant sound of a barking dog. He hoped there were no strays wandering the countryside. He knew no one would be at Ed's. It wasn't hunting season. He felt concerned a stray could come by and fight with his girls or, worse, bring in some disease at a time when he wanted to breed Mieke. He sure didn't need a case of rabies or parvovirus on his premises. He vowed to be on the lookout for signs of a stray while driving down the road.

He remembered his visit to Ed's with Jennifer Parker. He smiled when he thought of her wig. Why in the world does she think she needs to hide her femininity beneath a wig? He remembered how she looked as she stood in front of the window in his spare room. He wondered why he never thought of her as a woman before. He realized he thought of her as a psychic, an entity so different from anyone he knew he placed her in a class of her own.

He wondered if that was why she never married. Then he thought, I'm only assuming she's never been married. Jennifer knew so much about Glen. He often wondered how much she really knew. She told him many times she couldn't or, was that, wouldn't, spend time wandering around inside his head. He could never be quite sure.

He planned the next time he saw her to ask about her personal life. He wondered when their paths would cross again. He could sure use her help on the Slater homicide. Most of the time he waited until she found him with news of a case he was working on. Or his sergeant would call her in on a case. She almost never worked with the other cops. Sometimes, even though he didn't like it, his sergeant would pull him off of a case he was knee deep in to assist on a case where Jennifer was involved. One thing about it, she definitely sped up the investigation.

If she could help him find the body or the weapon he could nail Frank Slater. Maybe he should give her a call to see if she wanted to assist with this case.

He went back inside to fill his glass one more time. As he stepped back onto the porch his cell phone rang. He looked at the name on the caller ID on the screen. He chuckled to himself, "Why am I not surprised?" Then answered, "Jennifer, what's up?"

"I'm not sure. My thoughts for the evening turned to you. I learned many years ago to follow one's instincts. So I'm phoning you."

"I was about to call you." He looked at his watch. It was still early, only seven. "Have you had dinner yet?"

"No, I was planning to have tea and soup tonight. Are you proposing a better offer?"

"I'm working on a case that's not moving forward as quickly as I'd like. I thought maybe you might be able to lend me your skills."

"Where did you have in mind?"

"How about somewhere near your house so I don't keep you out too late?"

"Okay. Would Marie Callender's work for you?"

"I'll make it work. Give me forty-five minutes to get to your house. Oh, and nix the wig. You don't need to convince me you're a pro, just relax."

"I'll be waiting."

Glen gulped down the last of his bourbon and ran inside to slip on a clean shirt. He put the dogs out back. Soon he was ringing Jennifer's bell. When she opened the door her cat, Ming Ming, slipped out. Glen reached down to pick him up.

Jennifer grinned. "Not a cat man, are you?"

"Oh sure. I don't mind..." he stopped, knowing she might see through his comments. "I guess I like dogs better."

They shared a bottle of wine over dinner. Glen felt more relaxed around Jennifer now since she dressed more casually. He could almost forget she was a psychic.

"Can I ask you a personal question?"

"Yes, you may."

"Have you ever been married?"

"Yes, a while back."

"Can I ask what happened?"

"My son and my husband went white water rafting on a spring day twelve years ago. The currents were too strong. Their boat tipped over and in a split second I lost them both."

"I'm so sorry. I shouldn't have asked."

"No, Glen. That's quite all right. Time has eased the pain. Now you're wondering why I never remarried?"

"Actually, yes."

"Do you remember when we spent time in Omaha?"

"How can I forget? I've still got the ache in my arm to remind me."

"I apologize. I should say, do you remember when Paula's husband died and I saw him with her? I was able to share his messages with her."

"Yeah, I remember," he said as he popped a rather large piece of steak into his mouth. He swallowed a little sooner than he should have causing him to gulp his wine, easing the steak down.

"It would be extremely difficult for me to remarry when my husband and I shared so strong a love that it remains intact after he crossed over. We still communicate on a regular basis. He has told me many times to move on and find someone else, but knowing he is always with me is enough. I'll remain single until we can be together again."

Glen studied her face. He saw an expression he could not begin to understand nor describe. She didn't look sad, but her face bore a deeper look of something.

She broke his stare.

"This case you would like my assistance with?"

"I could use your help finding a body or the murder weapon. You choose. I'll be happy with either one," he teased.

He realized this is the first time he had such a lighthearted attitude around Jennifer.

"Oh, that's so kind of you Detective Karst, allowing me to choose."

"Here's the case. I'm sure this guy offed his wife. He has a hole in his alibi that I plan to get to the bottom of tomorrow. I can now prove he lied to me. She didn't show up for work one morning. Her co-workers called it in. No one had any idea where she may have gone. Her car is also missing. I found out their marriage wasn't what it seemed. When I searched the house I found the signs of a bloody death in their bedroom. The problem is no body and no weapon. This guy stands a strong chance of walking if I don't find more."

"Glen, I'm not sure I can help you. Remember I can't always pick up the information you may be looking for; I have to settle for what comes to me. Can you get me into the house?"

"At this point, only with his permission. We've already completed our investigation based on the search warrant."

"Okay. Can we drive by his house and park on the outside?"

"That we can do. How about tonight?"

Jennifer looked at her watch. It was already nine-thirty. She had hoped for an early evening. She has a book talk to give at the Tattered Cover Book store the next day.

She looked at Glen who had a hopeful expression on his face.

"Fine, tonight will be fine."

Glen, out of courtesy, glanced at her plate to be sure she had finished eating before he summoned their waiter.

He drove her to the Cherry Creek neighborhood where the Slater's shared a beautiful home. He parked two doors down.

Jennifer looked at the house. She felt nothing.

"Do you mind if we get out and take a stroll?"

"That'd be great."

He jumped out to run around the other side of his pickup to open the door for her. He offered her his hand as she stepped down from the tall pickup. Jennifer drove

Clinical Death

a Lincoln Continental, which sat much lower to the ground. She found it difficult to step down gracefully from Glen's truck.

As they strolled down the street, Glen pointed to the window on the east side of the house with pale pink draperies. There was a light on in the room. The figure of a man walked past the window. Glen recognized him as Mr. Slater.

Jennifer looked up at the window and the man— still nothing.

"I'm sorry Glen, I'm just not grasping anything."

They crossed the street to get a closer look. Along the edge of the intersection of the driveway and sidewalk Jennifer bent down to smell a rose. She closed her eyes as she inhaled the fragrance. Suddenly, she had a picture of Christine in her mind. It was Christine who planted the roses. Christine must've loved flowers because the yard was full of them.

"Glen, her body is outdoors, exposed to the elements and there are wildflowers near her."

Chapter 7

Glen noticed a pair of cops from the K-9 unit loading their dogs when he pulled up to work the next morning. He flagged them down.

"Karst, I heard you were back," said Paul.

"Can't keep me away."

"Is there something we can help you with? Everything okay with Mieke?" he asked.

"Sure, she's fine. No, she's actually great. Thanks again for making it possible for me to get her. Remember I told you I wanted to breed her some day?"

"Yeah."

"Well, that someday is here. She's in heat and I've been taking her in to the vet every other day to check her cycle. It's getting closer and I still haven't picked a stud. Is there one you'd suggest?"

"Bruno's a good stud. How about him? He can be one mean son of a bitch when we need him to be."

Bruno displayed a mostly black coat and face, his dark tan highlights, stocky build and longer hair made his one hundred thirty pounds of hyper intelligent presence even more ominous.

Glen smiled as he remembered a demonstration where Bruno snapped a two-by-six in half with one bite after a tap on the nose from Paul. Bruno remained on a sit-stay spitting the wood chips from his mouth and smiling at the crowd.

"Under other circumstances that would be great but I was going for more brains and less brute, if you get my drift. I'm living in a sleepy little community and I'm not sure if I'm keeping any of the pups. I'd feel bad if I had an aggressive litter that might hurt someone."

"That's all in the training, well, almost all."

"I know that, but I want to do all I can to guarantee a gentle nature, like Mieke."

He wanted to choose the stud based on physical characteristics. Mieke's black saddle, dark face with even highlights of tan and cream to match her sides and belly, made her gorgeous. Her demeanor around alpha males was appropriately submissive but, to the educated eye, it was clear she planned to have the last word.

"How about Valor, Dano's dog? I heard he stands him stud once in a while. You'd swear that dog is human, as smart as he is. He's one hell of a good drug dog, just like Mieke was."

"Hell, German Shepherds in general are smarter than most humans, give him a little credit," laughed Glen. "Where would I find Dano?"

"He's inside. I'll bet if you hurry you can catch him and Valor before they load out."

"Thanks, Paul. I'll do that."

Valor was certainly impressive in his own right— tall, lean and leggy, an image of his wolf heritage. Glen recalled the story that circulated around the department. Dano was called to an "abandoned" junkyard one night to see if Valor could hit on some drugs, specifically methamphetamine, so the narcotic agents could obtain a warrant. Shortly after they crossed the downed fence, two huge Rottweilers came from nowhere on a full run. Valor engaged and dispatched both while Dano and the boys were still drawing their guns. A snap of the fingers and "find" from Dano put Valor right back on task and meth he did find, a super lab buried deep below the singlewide office.

Glen darted in through the back door of the building in search of Dano and Valor. He didn't have far to go when he bumped into them getting ready to leave.

"Hey, Dano. Do ya have a second?"

"Glen, welcome back. What's up?" They shook hands warmly.

"Mieke's in heat and I wondered if you'd let me breed her to Valor?"

Clinical Death

"Hell yes, as long as I can have a pup or two from the mix. I helped train Mieke and she's one brilliant animal. I'd be honored to let Valor sire a litter with her. Just tell us where and when and we'll be there."

"She's getting close, probably next week. I'm using a little vet clinic in Wallace. I'll contact them and let them know I've found a local stud and see what they want to do. I'm not sure if they want a natural cover or an A.I."

"Valor's the man. I'm sure he wants to do the deed, none of this A.I. stuff for him."

"I'll see what the vets wanna do and get back to ya," said Glen.

He left Valor and Dano and walked to his division. He decided to put his neighbor's death out of his mind. This wouldn't be the first nor the last case where he knew something he couldn't prove. He had his own work piling up at the office. After his involvement in the Omaha situation, he decided it best to focus on the work at hand.

He called Frank.

"Mr. Slater, this is Detective Karst. I was wondering if you were free to stop by the station today. I have something to discuss with you."

"I don't think so, I'm pretty busy. If you have any news, I think you can tell me on the phone."

"I do have some news. Your wife didn't spend the night with you. She had a room at the Ramada Inn."

There was silence on the other end of the phone.

"If I told you about the fight we had, I'd be your number one suspect. I assumed she checked in with one of her boyfriends. After you found the blood in the bedroom I assumed they stopped by the house after I went to work. I didn't know how to get myself out of the web I weaved."

Glen wanted to give Frank the impression that he believed him.

"I guess that makes sense. Is there anything else you'd like to tell me that can help with the case? I understand your apprehension about changing your story, but now it's out in the open."

"No, that's it."

"Okay, thanks. I'll call you if anything turns up. Hope your kids are coping."

"It would help if her body turned up so we could all have a little closure."

"I hear you. We'll find her."

Glen checked the computer impound data as he had done every day since he began the case. Finally, another lead; security at the airport turned in a suspicious car. The report stated a 2005 Red Toyota Camry, registered to Frank and Christine Slater, had not been moved for thirty days. Denver city ordinance allows a vehicle to remain parked at the airport for no more than thirty days. Then the airport parking security will call it in to the NCIC and enter it on the national computer database accessible by all police departments. Then security will impound the car.

Glen was ecstatic; this could be a big break in the case. He called ahead asking them not to impound the car until he had a chance to go over it. He hurried to the airport impound lot with an investigative team.

The first thing Glen noticed was the position of the driver's seat. Christine stood five-foot-four without her shoes. The seat remained in the position for the last driver, back as far as possible. Christine couldn't have driven the car with the seat in that position.

Glen stood anxiously by as they opened the trunk.

He smiled when he saw a set of golf clubs. A closer examination of the trunk showed traces of blood and a few strands of broken hair matching the color of Christine's. Only a trained eye would have caught the faint evidence. Glen always carried a small flashlight for that reason. The trunk looked as though it had been thoroughly cleaned.

Glen studied the clubs.

"Anyone here a golfer?" he asked.

"I am", said one of the investigators.

"Okay, good," said Glen. "I don't play myself, but isn't it pretty standard for a putter to be included in each set?"

The young man who stepped forward to assist Glen said, "Well, yeah. You might have fewer irons or woods but it's nearly impossible to play a good game without your putter on the greens."

"Do you see a putter here?" asked Glen.

"No sir," he replied.

"Thanks."

More than ever, Glen was convinced that a golf club, more precisely a putter, belonging to Frank Slater had to be the weapon in question. Knowing Frank's putter was the missing weapon didn't bring him any closer to finding a body.

***

When Susie walked past the door of the exam room she stopped to watch Angie and Cal.

"What's up?" she asked.

She could tell they were concerned about the Cocker Spaniel on the table. Susie loved learning about new cases as long as they weren't too gruesome.

Angie shot a glance at Cal. Susie didn't need to hear this.

"This little guy's been killing Jan Gushard's chickens. She wants us to put him down," said Cal.

Immediately, Susie's eyes welled with tears and she ran down the hall.

Angie glared at Cal with a disapproving look.

"Hey, if she's gonna work here she has to toughen up and take the good with the bad."

"I guess. Do you want me to go fill the syringe?"

"Yes, let's get it over with."

Angie returned with a syringe filled with a pink fluid.

Cal injected the dog who slowly slid down onto the table motionless.

"I'll stay with him," said Angie.

"Make sure you check for a pulse."

"I know, I know. How many times have I helped you do this?"

"Too many. Now that you mention it, I don't think either Maria or Susie have assisted when they know you're in the building and not out on a farm call. Hell, I remember when Maria refused to help; she made me wait until you were back at the end of the day."

"I think that's because I told them if it was ever too much for them, I'd do it."

"So why is it that you can handle it so well?"

"I guess maybe all the years of watching animals die from accidents or being in pain, this seems like the best way to go if you have to."

"I agree. I hope when the time comes for me, someone slips me a drug to end my pain and suffering."

Cal left Angie alone to deal with the death and disposal of the Cocker Spaniel's body.

Becky found Dr. Jensen in her office.

"Detective Karst called. He said he found a stud dog and wanted to know if you were planning a natural cover or an A.I.?"

"Call him back and tell him we'll do whatever he and the stud owner want. Tell him natural is always good but the best chances are with surgical insemination. His dog is young so if she misses we can always try again in seven months or so."

Becky called Glen at the end of the day when she made her follow-up calls. Angie and Maria had taken off early. For once, the schedule was light in the afternoon so Susie and only one of the vets stayed until closing.

Glen answered his phone then walked out into his yard with the dogs while he spoke to Becky.

"I think I might like to try the surgical insemination if that's the best guarantee. Janet convinced me not to have puppies in the winter so if I miss this heat it'll be over a year before I can try again."

"Okay, I'll tell her."

"Wait. What do I have to do next?"

"Keep bringing her in for blood draws and on the day they say she's ready, have the stud here. They'll collect him at the clinic. You might see if he can be collected at home first just to empty any old sperm out of him."

"Wow, you know your stuff," said Glen.

Becky blushed on the other end of the phone.

Clinical Death

"Not really, I just have to pass this message on to breeders occasionally and some of it sticks."

Glen played ball with Mieke, always throwing it just ahead of her so she could catch it on the run. Taffy should be ready to go in tomorrow to have her cast removed if she healed properly.

Suddenly, Cheyenne and Mieke pricked their ears to the sound of dogs wailing.

"Damn," said Glen. It sounded like there might be more than one stray dog in the area. "Come on girls. Get in the house."

He tucked them away inside then went to investigate. He took his pistol with him just in case he might be dealing with rabid animals. He walked to end of his property line. The dog's barking and howling grew louder as he approached Ed's place. He parted the barbed wire fence and slipped through to the other side.

Once on Ed's property, he remained alert for the dogs. They were silent. He stood for a moment in the bushes and overgrown trees in the pasture where Ed kept his cows. He waited. Still nothing. Just as he turned to head back to his farm, they started in again.

He walked toward Ed's house while his eyes scanned the ground for cow pies and the brush for dogs. He crossed the pasture then climbed the wooden corral fence. His best boots sank down into the mud from the leaky stock tank.

"Damn it," he said, as he pulled one boot out at a time. The mud pulled hard, trying to hold on.

He searched the ground for the driest area to walk when the dogs started in again. He thought, the hell with these boots. Then he jogged toward the sound of the dogs with the mud easing its hold as the ground became drier.

He climbed over the corral fence putting him in the barnyard. He stopped to listen for the dogs.

"They have to be in the horse barn," he whispered to himself.

He searched the yard for signs of another person or vehicle. He appeared to be alone. He went to the barn door and slowly opened it just a crack so he could look inside. In the darkness within the barn he could see nothing. He opened the door wider, allowing daylight to creep in. He stepped inside, giving his eyes a chance to adjust to the low level of light.

The dogs began to whine excitedly. He could tell they were in one of the stalls. He opened the doors as widely as possible to allow more light inside. Fumbling for the light switch but he realized the electricity had been disconnected after Ed died.

He walked over to the dogs who wriggled and whined when they jumped on the stall boards with chicken wire attached. They licked Glen's fingers as he stuck them through the wire.

Clinical Death

"What're you guys doing here?"

He checked to see if they had food and water.

"Someone's taking good care of you. But what in the hell are you doing here?"

The opened bag of dog food against the wall outside of the stall was the same brand as the neatly stacked empty bags he'd discovered on his farm.

Opening the stall door slightly and he squeezed his body inside. He noticed the same type of toys he'd found in his barn. He squatted down to play tug with the black Cocker Spaniel and the Australian Shepherd. Sunlight fell across the shepherd's face from the window above Glen's head.

"What the hell? You're supposed to be dead."

Glen ran his fingers through the coat just as he had done on the day he startled Angie. When the dog calmed down from the excitement of someone to play with, Glen studied the its face more intently.

"You are the same dog. What're you doing here?"

Glen's eyes scanned the barn for anything else out of the ordinary before he said his goodbyes to the dogs and headed home.

He decided to take the road to avoid the muddy corrals. Strolling along the road to his house not one car or truck passed him. The sunset, the sound of birds, and the gentle hum of a tractor in the distance brought him back to his childhood. He savored the smells of springtime in the country. He wished he could take his dogs for long walks, but it wouldn't be fair to Taffy, with her bad leg, or Mieke, once she became heavy in whelp. The walks would have to wait until the puppy project was behind him then the girls and he would wander around the countryside in the crisp fall air.

Early the next morning, Phil had an Vizsla on the exam table while he explained the medical facts of the case to the owners. Maria helped with the dog who had a closed uterine infection or pyometra. She had not been spayed and had a heat cycle a few weeks earlier. The owner noticed the dog became lethargic and quit eating. The pus-filled uterus required an emergency spay and a strong regime of antibiotics to save the dog's life. The dog belonged to their daughter who had gone off to college. The parents, not wanting a dog especially when they discovered the medical procedure, decided to euthanize her. They'd explain it to their daughter later.

Maria went to find Angie. She hoped she hadn't left yet for the country with Cal or Janet. The owners wanted to be there when the dog was euthanized so they could inform their daughter they remained with her until the end—hoping to ease the blow.

Angie and Janet were loading vet supplies on the truck when Maria caught up to them.

"Angie, I'll go out to the country if you want to handle a dog getting euthanized," said Maria.

Clinical Death

Angie looked at Janet.

"Sure, go ahead." She turned to Maria, "If you're coming, hurry up and grab your stuff. I'm already running late. We've got three hundred head to vaccinate."

Maria hated working cattle, but if it meant getting out of the Vizsla situation, she'd gladly make the switch.

Phil liked working with Angie when they had clients in the room during the procedure. He knew she had enough experience to handle the dog while he comforted the clients.

She handed the syringe to him then held the dog while he injected it. The dog slid down onto the table and the wife began to cry. Phil encouraged them to step out into the hall with him while Angie took the body out the other door to the back.

Phil escorted the couple to the door answering questions. He glanced up at the clock after they pulled away.

Stacey said, "I'm glad you noticed. You and Cal are going to be late for your meeting. I think he went ahead already."

"Where's Janet?"

"She's in the country. Who should I call in case of an emergency?"

"Call me, I guess, but only for an emergency."

He changed from his scrubs into street clothes then popped back to the front desk.

"You might as well send everyone else home. Keep one tech."

"Okay, see ya later."

"Did I hear him say we can go home?" asked Angie.

"Well, he said someone. It'll either be you or Susie since Maria's with Dr. Jensen."

"It'll be me. I was going to ask to take off early anyway. I have a doctor appointment."

"Okay, see ya tomorrow."

Angie left through the back door where her pickup was parked. She drove home to make her call.

"Dr. Bradley, this is Angie. I'm heading in early. Is tonight the night Nancy's coming?"

"No, she'll be here tomorrow. Why don't you wait until then?"

"I can't."

"What'd you have?"

"I've got a female Vizsla with a fever of one hundred and five. She's got a closed pyometra."

"How soon will you be here?"

"Give me a little over two hours."

"Are you going to assist with the surgery?"

"Yeah, sure, isn't that what we usually do?"

"I'm just checking. I'll have a room ready."

Angie stopped by Ed's farm to pick up the Cocker Spaniel and the Australian Shepherd. She gave the Vizsla a shot of antibiotics and a tranquilizer to relax her before the trip.

When she reached Dr. Bradley's office in Sterling, they unloaded the two healthy dogs into the outside kennel runs. Then they began working on the Vizsla. The surgery went well, but the infection had been there long enough Dr. Bradley was unsure how well the dog would recover.

"How long before she can travel?" asked Angie.

"She might have to stay here for a few days and then we'll have to move her out before my techs get suspicious. Can you come back for her? Nancy won't be back for a couple more weeks."

"I think I can set her up at my new place for a while until she's ready to travel."

Nancy showed up the following evening after hours.

"Wow, what a pretty face on this one. These markings are so unique," she said as she played with the Australian Shepherd. I think we should shave this Cocker before we send it to its new home. I'll have my mom clean her up. I'm not sure the family I've got lined up would be too thrilled to see all the mats and weeds in her coat."

"Thanks, Nancy. I'd hoped you were gonna say that. Angie and I can't clip hair unless we're shaving them bald. I'm glad your mom's so good at it."

"So that's it, just the two?"

"I have an Vizsla but she's not ready to travel. Angie's gonna have to look after her until you come back."

Glen stopped by the clinic before closing time.

"Sorry I missed my appointment earlier today but I couldn't get away."

"That's okay. Maria can still draw the blood and read the test results. She'll write them down for the doctors. Then we'll give you a call," said Stacey.

"I have Taffy with me. I hoped someone could take her cast off.
Is Angie here?"

"No, she's off for the afternoon. She had a doctor appointment. Can Maria help you?"

"Sure if she can take the cast off, but I wanted to ask Angie about a dog that I saw her with the other day."

Stacey, with a curious look on her face, said, "What dog?"

"Oh nothing, just a patient here. I'll catch her next time."

Maria escorted Glen and Mieke into an exam room. She drew blood and Glen watched as she ran the test. He learned how to read the results himself.

"We're almost there," he said.

"Yep, you're right. I'm guessing she's ovulating. They're gonna want to breed her probably on Sunday if you're doing the surgical.

Clinical Death

"Great timing. Dano doesn't work on Sundays and neither do I. I'll give you a call and we can set up an appointment. While I'm here, can you take off Taffy's cast or do you want one of the vets to see her first?"

"Why don't you bring her along on Sunday."

Although the clinic is only open Monday through Friday and half a day on Saturday, when timed procedure situations arise like this insemination or emergencies, one of the vets opens the clinic to take care of the client. Small town vet clinics with service twenty-four seven are a dying breed.

The dogs and Glen headed home. He couldn't resist stopping at Ed's to check on the mystery dogs in the barn. He made his dogs stay in the back of the pickup in the camper shell.

He looked around first to be sure he was alone. He could tell by the tire tracks in the dirt someone had been there since the previous night. He made a mental note of the tread design.

He wondered why they were so quiet as he opened the door widely and stepped inside.

They were gone. Water remained in the bowls and food in the dishes but, no dogs. He leaned against the wall studying the open pens as he bit his lip in thought.

What difference should it make to him if someone hid dogs in the barn at Ed's place? No harm apparently had been done. Whoever it was must have moved over to Ed's when Glen bought his farm and moved in.

If the dogs are being well cared for why should he bother himself with it? Because he cannot walk away from anything the least bit suspicious without an adequate explanation—as a detective, he just couldn't let it rest. Dead dogs coming back to life, live dogs missing, a dead neighbor's unexplainable death and then his official work with a missing body and a missing murder weapon increased his stress.

"Living in the country's not quite like I remembered," he mumbled as he closed the barn door.

Chapter 8

Glen and his dogs spent a peaceful Saturday morning exploring the farm. He put all thoughts of crime out of his mind as he watched the dogs romping through the tall pasture grasses. The extra rainfall this spring encouraged the wildflowers to burst into bloom.

He came across a gentle rise in the ground facing the morning sun. Lying back in the deep lush grass to watch the clouds pass overhead, he plucked petals from wildflower blossoms growing next to him. As he closed his eyes, he felt the tension leaving his body. The sun warmed his face as he enjoyed the aroma of crushed green grass and the fragrant flowers. He drifted off into a near sleep state. As he lie there he could hear the buzzing of insects, but none landed on him. He listened to the unmistakable sound of a breeze through pine needles. He could hear the birds all around him in the trees. Relaxing more deeply he could hear the soft flowing sound of water in the stream. Occasionally, he heard the plop of an insect being snatched from the surface of the water by a small fish.

The sides of his mouth curled slightly as he enjoyed the sensation of being one with nature. How different this was from the rat race of the office and city traffic. Taffy brought Glen back to the present moment when she stood next to him licking his face. He jumped with a start then opened his eyes to see the brown-eyed Taffy wagging her tail.

Roughing up her coat he looked behind him to see where the other dogs had gone. They were still snuffling through the grasses. Glen leaped to his feet. Where were the trees and the stream? Where were the birds and insects he heard? He found himself completely surrounded by pasture grasses and wildflowers, but no trees, no brook, no insects buzzing. Had he slipped into a dream state?

No, that's impossible, everything was so intensely vivid. Positive he had been awake sensing all of nature surrounding him, he turned in a complete circle hoping to find an explanation for what just happened. Then he dropped back down to the ground bending his knees slightly, resting his arms on his legs; he surveyed the area. He sat perfectly still to see if the insects would return. Closing his eyes, he tried to listen more intently to bring back the sounds he heard earlier—nothing.

He sat there for the better part of an hour confused as to what he experienced. He called the dogs and went to the house for lunch hoping food would create a distraction.

As he prepared a sandwich his thoughts turned to Jennifer Parker, remembering the time she convinced him to relax and let his mind wander. He remembered envisioning the railroad tracks where the two missing girls were found before he received the call. Now that he gave it some thought, he realized he experienced the same almost asleep, dreamy feeling. Could this be what Jennifer refers to when she mentions a meditative state? Did he just have a vision?

No, he thought, too much stress. I just dozed off for a little while in the peaceful setting under the morning sun. He took a bite of his sandwich. He failed to notice he still stood at the counter, not having taken his plate to the table.

"That had to be it," he said out loud, as if hearing it would help convince himself.

He set his sandwich down and wiped his mouth.

"Son of a bitch, I smelled wildflowers, I heard a stream, I heard the rustle of pine trees, I had bugs buzzing around and heard birds. Jennifer said Christine's body was out in the open near wildflowers. Christine's body is in the mountains."

Glen nervously paced the kitchen. He felt a rush of excitement when he realized he probably sensed the site where Christine's body lie exposed to the elements. What he experienced was through his senses of sound and smell, not vision. How could that help him? He didn't see the spot or know what to look for. There would be hundreds of places in the mountains where one would find streams, pine trees and wildflowers.

"Great," he mumbled. "I finally do what Jennifer's been trying to teach me to do and I can't use it."

Glen's pace quickened, always in control and self-assured, confidence ruled his life. He felt he could do whatever he put his mind to but this...this was so uncontrollable. How can he learn to master what he doesn't understand? It's not like he could run to the library and check out a book on developing his psychic abilities...or could he?

"This is insane. Jennifer writes books on psychic abilities. I can't believe I didn't think of that sooner. Just goes to show I'm not really very psychic after all," he chuckled to himself as he dialed Jennifer's number.

"Jennifer, Glen. I was wondering if you write any of your psychic books for dummies?"

"What?" she laughed.

"I'm wondering how difficult your books are to understand for, say, someone like me who's a rookie on the subject."

"Okay, Glen, what happened?"

"What do you mean?"

Clinical Death

"I know you well enough to know you wouldn't be calling me asking for written advice on psychic powers unless something happened."

"That's just it, Jennifer. I'm not sure what happened."

"Would you like to come over and talk about it? I can show you the books I've written and numerous others from a multitude of competent authors on the subject. I still have my text books from my school in London."

"Would you mind if I stopped by in the next hour or so? Did you have plans? I don't want to just barge in without advance warning."

"Well, Detective Karst, I had planned a shopping day with a lady friend of mine and for some reason I called her and cancelled. My day is clear. Please, come over directly. We'll begin our work to solve your dilemma."

While Jennifer waited for Glen to arrive, she sorted through her library of books on paranormal behavior, channeling, visions and psychic phenomenon. She scanned through the pages not wanting to find anything too advanced or difficult that might overwhelm her friend.

Glen rang the bell.

"Welcome to my home, Glen. Please come in."

He followed her into the dining room. She arranged an assortment of books for him to peruse.

"May I get you something to drink?" she asked.

"An empty glass would be fine. I brought my own."
He took his flask of bourbon from inside his jacket pocket
and placed it on the table amid the books.

Jennifer returned with a cup of hot tea and one
empty glass for Glen. He had already begun thumbing
through the books.

"Why don't we begin with you explaining to me
what happened," she suggested.

"You know I wouldn't tell this to just anyone."

"I understand and I promise you I will never reveal
what you tell me to your co-workers when I'm working a
case with them."

Glen hadn't even considered her telling the guys at
work. He paused to think it over, then realized he could
trust Jennifer.

He poured a drink, took a big swallow and began,
"I was in my pasture with my dogs soaking up some sun.
I was lying in the tall grass. I'm not sure if I fell asleep or
not, but it felt so real."

"What felt real?" she asked.

"Everything. I smelled grass and flowers. Those I
know were real, then with my eyes closed I heard a stream
with small fish grabbing bugs and I heard the sound of
wind in pine trees and I heard birds."

"I'm not quite sure I understand, Glen. What was
unusual about experiencing those sensations?"

Clinical Death

"Nothing, except there are no trees, especially pine trees, in my pasture and definitely no stream or brook. I know there are bugs but when I opened my eyes I sure didn't see any."

He took another swallow from his glass.

"Glen, it appears to me you had an out-of-body experience during the day."

"What's that mean? During the day?"

"Well, many, many people leave their physical bodies while they sleep. Actually, we all do, but very few ever remember it or think of it as anything other than a dream. You see, your conscious mind is holding you back from seeing beyond what is right in front of you, especially someone like you who sees the world in black and white.

"A person's soul is made up of energy, as is their body. You already know from your science classes in school everything within the universe is nothing more than energy. I'm not great at defining science, but I do know everything is made up of atoms and atoms are made up of electrons, protons and neutrons—basically energy. All substances vibrate at different frequencies, which is why we have so many different elements or physical properties around us.

"One of the easiest examples to explain is water. Everyone knows it's made of hydrogen and oxygen. At room temperature the water appears still, but electrons are in a continuous state of vibration. When you increase the heat around water the atoms go wild, increasing their speed, creating more heat from the motion causing the water to boil. Now, the opposite is also true when you slow down the movement of the atoms, they become so sluggish the water freezes. One has to merely excite the electrons again and the ice melts to return to the natural state of water."

"What does that have to do with me?" asked Glen.

"I'm merely pointing out the extremes in atoms. Your body vibrates at a different frequency than you soul. Your soul is who you are and it is distinct from anyone else. Your soul is a much lighter frequency and when you sleep, it can rise above your heavier body and escape its confines for short periods of time."

"You mean, like the people who say they rose up to the ceiling in the hospital to watch the doctors working on their dead bodies, only to return to them and wake up alive?"

"That's it exactly. Some people can relax themselves into a meditative state and facilitate the departure while the body is alive and healthy in a quiet state. That is what I believe you experienced today."

Glen slid back in his chair. "Holy Shit. Oh, excuse me, Jennifer."

"No need for apologies, I've heard worse. Remember, during my lifetime I've been many places both consciously and subconsciously where people are not always, shall I say... nice."

Glen stared off at the wall behind the table as he thought about what Jennifer had told him.

"Now, we need to discover where you went," said Jennifer. "And why you went there. Do you have any of your hunches?"

"Yeah, I actually do have an idea. I think I might have been where that missing woman's body is. Remember, I took you by her house and all you could sense was that she was outside near wildflowers? I think I went there. Oh hell, listen to me, will ya? I sound like a real ass, don't I?"

"Are you saying when I tell you what I sense or see, you think of me as an ass?"

Glen, shocked to hear such language from Jennifer, fumbled for an apology, "No, that's not what I meant. I meant coming from me it sounds sort of, well...far-fetched."

"If you think you were there then I'd be willing to bet you were there."

"Yeah, but how do we find out where there is?" he asked.

"I'm not quite sure. For me, I have visions so I can tell people about landmarks, but you don't seem to have those facts so let's work with the ones you do have."

"How?"

"First, let's get you to relax. Come in here."

Glen followed Jennifer into a dimly lit room. She had drawn the heavy draperies over the windows. She walked around the room lighting candles and incense.

"Come sit here in my favorite chair. Do you like soft music or the sound of trickling water? I have many CDs of sounds or I can plug in my waterfall over in the corner to help relax you."

Glen obediently followed her to the chair.

"Let's not have any sounds. Since sounds are all I can remember I don't want to be confused."

"That's very wise. I'm going to leave you alone for about fifteen minutes. I want you to concentrate on all that you felt in your pasture then I'll come back and we can talk about it."

Glen fidgeted in the chair trying to get comfortable. "This is insane," he mumbled. He closed his eyes and tried to think back. He knew this wasn't going to work.

Jennifer returned to the room.

"I thought you were going to wait fifteen minutes," said Glen.

"I know, but thirty minutes seemed more appropriate."

"Thirty minutes, no way. You couldn't have been gone more than two or three."

Jennifer smiled. "Let's talk. Can you tell by the sound of the pine trees if there are several or only a few?"

Glen thought for a moment, "Only a few."

"Do they surround you?"

"They're behind me."

"Good. Now how large is the stream? Is the water rushing?"

"No, it's quiet, barely moving. It doesn't sound very deep and the fish sound small. Maybe it's only four or five feet wide."

"The insects, are they bees...?"

"No, they sound like large flies," he cut in.

"Where's the stream located?"

"In front of me. I can feel the sun coming from the same direction as the stream."

"Where are you lying?"

"In the grass, no...yes, in the grass, but its colder than grass and harder...no something hard is above me, but the sun can come through in spots. Oh, it's no use. I'm not getting anywhere."

"I think you did just fine, Glen." She handed a drawing to him.

He marveled at yet another talent she had that he was unaware of. He saw a mountain scene with a shallow stream, a shoreline with boulders and rocks with a few pine trees behind the rock formation. The sun shone across the water landing upon a pile of rocks that were stacked manually rather than by nature.

"How did you get this from what I said?"

"I went there with you. As you talked, I looked. Glen, this is more like a hiking path in the mountains. See these stacked rocks. I believe the body is beneath them. The rocks are facing east. There were no roads or you would've mentioned vehicles driving by."

"Jennifer, this could be anywhere."

"I know, would you like to go for a drive in the mountains?"

"Yes, but without a plan we could drive for weeks or months and not find the right trail," said Glen.

"Oh, come on. Where's your sense of adventure?"

They drove for hours and neither of them had any feelings or sense of the direction where Christine's body lie.

"I'd better get you home," said Glen.

"I'm sorry this didn't help much," responded Jennifer.

As they turned the corner to Jennifer's house, a folder filled with papers slid off of the dashboard spilling across the floor. Jennifer reached down for them.

"No, just leave them. I'll gather them up when I drop you off."

He pulled in front of her house then ran around to her side as he always did to open the door for her. He walked her safely to her door then left. He picked up the papers from the floor and tossed them onto the seat. He gathered them into a messy stack then drove home.

Clinical Death

He set the folder on the kitchen counter and fed the dogs. He put a frozen pizza in the oven, poured a glass of bourbon and sorted through the papers to reorganize them. The folder contained the information he had on the Slater case. As he restacked the emails into the separate piles for each of the women Frank had written to, he skimmed over them.

Frank bragged to one of the women about what an avid hiker he is. Glen laughed, "Yeah, just like the pro golfer that you are!"

He saw the pattern developing. Whenever a woman expressed an interest in something Frank was an instant expert.

"Hey, wait a minute," he said. He searched through the papers for the email conversation about hiking. The woman mentioned she loved to hike, he answered with how much he loved it. She mentioned her favorite spots, then he mentioned his. Glen couldn't believe his eyes. Is there a remote chance this guy might be describing a spot he's actually familiar with? Could he have dumped Christine's body there?

He scoured through the email thread on the hiking topic and found names of roads and paths. He described how he liked to leave the main trail and go off on his own. Glen cleared a large spot on the table with both arms, sending papers flying and almost spilling his drink. The buzzer went off for the pizza. He looked at the oven with the *not now* look. He rushed to the oven, turned it off, opened the door and almost grabbed the pizza with his bare hands. He jerked the towel from the door handle and took out the pizza, dropping it on the kitchen counter then returned to the work at hand.

He spread the hiking emails containing directions out onto the table and began to draw a map. He ran to his den and grabbed an atlas. Looking up the area in the Rocky Mountains just outside of Denver. He found the same highways and roads listed.

"The bastard might lead me to the body yet."

He grabbed a flashlight, extra batteries and the map. He looked back into the kitchen as he prepared to dart out of the door. His stomach reminded him he hadn't eaten today. He stacked four slices of pizza one on top of the other and left.

He sped down the highway back to Denver devouring the pizza slices before he was outside of his county. This time of night traffic was light for Denver.

The weather was perfect and he was blessed with a nearly full moon to light the dark shadows of the mountain roads. He followed his hand-drawn map until he had to leave his pickup behind. He had more difficulty once he was off of the road trying to decide the direction Frank had taken.

The directions on Frank's emails were too vague. After hours of wandering around, Glen stopped to regroup his thoughts. He checked his watch. Two o'clock in the morning and he was out alone looking for a body based on his gut instinct and a liar's directions. Something urged him to keep going. He backtracked and started down different trails, exiting them several times along the way to search for the secluded area Frank wrote about.

As the sun came up he got his bearings for direction. He found a stream that matched the description he and Jennifer had talked about. He followed it for miles. He found nothing. He stopped to rest on a boulder to check his cuts and scratches from hiking through the brush in the dark, grateful it was still too early for mosquitoes. He stretched his arms up over his head clasping his fingers together to help pull him into the stretch. His eyes caught sight of his watch.

It was nearly eight o'clock.

"Oh, shit. Mieke. Her appointment's in one hour."

He had no idea how long it would take him to hike back to his pickup. He couldn't make it to the clinic even if he left right this moment. He checked his cell phone—no signal.

He climbed out of the brush to higher ground. He turned in a circle looking at his cell phone.

"Wait, there's a signal. I hope it's strong enough."

He keyed in Dr. Jensen's phone number.

She didn't answer. His phone was about to die. All he could do would be to leave a quick message and hope for the best.

"Janet, Glen. Send Angie to pick up Mieke and Taffy. I'm on a case, can't make it in. Dano will be at the clinic with Valor at nine..." the phone died.

"Damn," said Glen, suppressing the urge to toss the phone into the water.

He looked toward the path, trying to choose which way to go next. Tired and hungry he decided to wander without much thought to which direction he headed. He walked to the water's edge to splash cold water onto his face.

He wiped his face on his sleeve then sat down to look at Jennifer's map. Once again, he admired her ability to sketch. He noticed her talent for details.

He looked at her mountains in the background. Most people would draw a string of triangular shapes to indicate the mountains off in the distance but not Jennifer. As he studied the drawing, he noticed the contour of her mountains. He stepped out to widen his view. He saw the same unusually shaped peaks across the water from where he stood. The shapes were the same but the angle was all wrong. He looked up and down the stream trying to find a spot to stand where he could line up the drawing in the same direction.

Clinical Death

He felt he was close but couldn't quite get the angle he wanted. He continued to search for two more hours. He knew he should head back to his truck but the same drive that kept him going throughout the night caused him to proceed.

He stopped to rethink his plan. Sitting down to study the mountains again, he realized the angle was better when he was closer to the ground. Of course, if he were seeing and feeling it from Christine's vantage point, it would be from the ground.

He heard the wind rush through the pine trees; he turned his head when he heard a small fish grab an insect from the water. He felt the sun on his face as he looked at the water.

Along the water's edge he found a small trail leading to the west into dense trees and brush. He followed the path. The sun shining from behind him caused a glisten up ahead on the ground. At first he thought it was a beer can shining in the sunlight but then realized the beam was too long.

He pushed branches out of his way as he went for the glistening object.

A golf club—the missing putter. He took off his jacket and draped it over the putter so he could locate it again. Removing his camera from his pocket he began to process the scene. Then he began to part the brush looking for Christine's body, all senses on high alert.

He looked for roosting birds that would feast on the insects feeding and breeding on the decomposing body. Drag marks, animal tracks—everything was important. A little breeze would help.

His heart raced; he knew he was close. He stopped and faced the sun. He couldn't see it through the brush. This wasn't the right spot. He went further upstream where the path widened. He saw orange, yellow and blue wildflowers in clusters where the brush thinned. His eyes scanned the area quickly looking for a pile of rocks as his pulse raced.

He followed the path around one more turn and there was a pile of rocks abuzz with flies and the unmistakable smell. A decomposing human body is so different from the smell of any other dead animal. The stench caused him to take a handkerchief from his pocket to cover his nose and mouth as he removed one stone at a time. He planned when he was finished at the scene to throw away his clothes. After only a few stones had been removed he saw the hand of a body with rotting flesh and insects squirming in and out of the body tissue—maggots so large Glen could hear them feeding.

Chapter 9

The noon sun shone upon the remains of Christine Slater as Glen backtracked with his camera. Anyone would be able to find the spot from his photos. With power for his phone available at his truck he summoned the crew. The crime scene investigators carefully removed the remainder of the rocks. Her body had been wrapped with black trash bags before being dumped at this remote site. The weight of the rocks and the small animals making small tears had allowed the bag to become infested with carcass-eating insects.

An exhausted Glen supervised the investigation, anxious for every detail to be handled properly. He slipped under the yellow crime scene tape anchored to nearby trees, glistening in the sun as it swayed gently in breeze. He went to the CSI supply vehicle in desperate need of a cup of coffee.

Bill arrived shortly after the CSI team.

"What happened to you?" he asked.

"What?" asked Glen.

"Your face and arms. Did you tangle with a wild cat or something?"

Glen hardly noticed the scratches and cuts on his face, neck and arms.

Bill motioned for one of the EMTs at the scene to come to them.

"Can you administer a little first-aid to this guy?"

"I tried but he wouldn't let me."

"He'll let you now," said Bill.

"I'm fine," said Glen as they both walked away.

Glen had already made a salve of native bee pollen and the sandy river mud from the stream. He always took bee pollen if it looked like it would be a long night. One could live on the pollen and it requires little space. The salve served as a fringe benefit of the pollen.

Glen sipped the coffee as he watched Christine's remains being carried away. There was nothing more he could do at the crime scene. He found the body, located the weapon and the remainder of the team scoured the grounds for any other bits of evidence.

"How in the hell did you find her?" asked Bill.

Glen looked down at his boots as he thought about how to respond. He wasn't ready for the department to know the whole truth. He chose to credit Jennifer Parker with some of the work.

"Jennifer Parker..."

"Oh, here we go again. That damned psychic."

Clinical Death

Ignoring Bill's skepticism Glen went on, "Jennifer Parker told me we'd find her outside where wildflowers grow. I was reading back through the emails Slater wrote to his girlfriends and ran across a thread about hiking. I jotted down his details and made a map of sorts to find the body. It took me all night, but I finally stumbled across her. Actually, I found the golf club first. I knew I was close. When I got near the spot I could smell her. Son of a bitch is done. All I need are his prints on the club and no one else's; otherwise I'll take the circumstantial case to the jury. Either way, he's toast."

At the pathology lab they were unable to find anything on the body to help prove Glen's case, other than the impression in the skull matching that of the putter in question. Her body was too badly decomposed to find skin or blood beneath her nails. Dental records confirmed the body was that of Christine Slater.

He waited for the fingerprint results. He sat at his desk waiting for the phone to ring. He tapped his foot impatiently on the floor.

"Ring, damn it, ring," he growled.

As he stood to get a cup of coffee the phone rang.

"Karst."

"We've got him, Glen. The prints were crystal clear and a perfect match."

"Any other prints?"

"Not a one."

"Yes!" said Glen out loud knowing the defense would simply say the real killer wore gloves.

Glen previously drafted the body of the arrest warrant and it waited on the screen of his computer for the results of the fingerprint analysis to be added then off to the D.A.'s office then the judge.

With warrant in hand Glen grabbed his jacket from the back of the chair and Bill followed him out of the office. Together they drove to Frank's building. They took the elevator up to his floor. The receptionist tried to stop them. Bill flashed his badge.

Glen burst into Frank's office, startling him.

"Frank Slater, you're under arrest for the murder of your wife, Christine Slater."

Bill read him his rights as Glen cuffed him and escorted him past his co-workers. Glen breathed a sigh of relief as he drove through the city with Frank cuffed in his backseat. He knew, without a shadow of a doubt, he was going to pay for what he had done to his wife.

Dano found Glen at his desk.

"What the hell happened to you yesterday?" he asked.

Glen looked up.

"Fighting crime, facing dangers and saving lives."

Dano smiled at the familiar ranting of the seasoned cop.

Clinical Death

"I was up in the mountains all night on a case and when I realized how late in the morning it was I knew I couldn't make it back down. I'm sorry that you had to go to the clinic for nothing."

"It wasn't for nothing. We got Mieke bred."

"But how? Did Dr. Jensen get my message? I thought my phone died."

"She must've because when I got there Mieke and some little brown dog were there. The procedure was pretty slick. They anesthetized your dog and made a really small incision, no more than an inch or so in her side. Then they collected semen from Valor in a syringe. She injected the semen directly into the uterus through the opening and sewed her back up. I never had a clue they could do things like that."

"How's Mieke?"

"She was fine. She woke up while I was there. Then they took a cast off of the little dog. She's not yours, is she?"

"Yeah, long story. I guess I saved her life by giving her a home. Where're my dogs now?"

"They said they were going to keep them at the clinic until you picked them up. I gotta get to work."

"Hey, thanks again, Dano. I hope we get a nice sized litter."

"Remember, I want the pick of two pups."

"They're yours," said Glen.

Patricia A. Bremmer

Glen left work an hour early so he could pick up
his dogs. When he opened the door to the clinic, he
noticed the staff huddled around the front counter. By
the whispering and body language he knew something
quite important must have been going on.

Angie saw Glen then darted off to the back room.

"What's up? Is Angie okay?"

"What? Angie? Oh, yeah. Phil just called for her
to hurry to the back. He had a snarling cat he needed help
holding down," said Stacey.

"I thought maybe it was something serious," said
Glen.

"Talk about serious," said Stacey.

Glen knew he was about to get an earful.

"What?" he asked.

"Louis Boyle was found dead."

"I'm sorry. Who is Louis Boyle?"

"You probably don't know him," said Stacey.

"What happened?" asked Glen.

"His wife, Rosemary, just got back from visiting
their daughter in London. She's been going to school
there. Anyway, when she got home yesterday afternoon
she couldn't find Louis. She stopped by here to pick up
her Schnauzer, Libby. Some of her neighbors were here
when she arrived, she asked if they'd seen Louis."

"Oh, I remember her. I was here with Mieke when
she dropped off her dog."

156

"Well, yeah. Anyway, she went back home and made a few calls. No one saw him."

"I thought she said he was going with her," said Glen.

"He was supposed to, but then at the last minute he stayed behind. His truck was home but there was no sign of him. The neighbors all came over when he didn't show up for supper. His tractors were parked. They took flashlights and started looking everywhere for him.

"Sheriff Tate sat down with Rosemary to ask her some questions. When they found out Louis stayed behind because he wanted to work on his grain pit they grabbed their flashlights and headed out there.

"According to Angie..."

"Why was Angie there?"

"Everyone was there by nightfall helping with the search.

"Anyway, Angie said they looked all around the grain pit then noticed the door on top of the pit had a pile of irrigation pipes on it. The men moved the pipes. I guess there must've been over thirty pipes on it.

"When they opened the door and shined the flashlight down there they saw Louis. He was all crumpled up in the corner like he'd been cold or something. Sheriff Tate climbed the ladder twenty feet down to the bottom of the pit. He said Louis was dead.

"They had Doc Wilson go down to confirm it before they moved the body. They had to lower a stretcher down to get him out. Doc said he died from lack of food and water and exposure on the cold nights we had."

"How'd the irrigation pipes get on top of the door?" asked Glen.

"Oh, I don't know. Can you imagine being locked down there with no food and water until you died? I don't know why he didn't just use his cell phone."

"He probably didn't have a signal twenty feet down in a concrete pit," said Glen.

"Yeah, whatever, but can you imagine how gross he must've looked. But then you probably see dead bodies all the time in your line of work."

"More than I'd like to," said Glen. "Why is it no one missed him until now?"

"Everyone thought he went with his wife."

"That means he didn't show up at the coffee shop from the first day she left," said Glen.

"Oh, I don't know. I guess," said Stacey. "I wonder how Rosemary's doing?"

Glen didn't want to pursue the discussion any further.

"Are my dogs ready to go?"

"Sure, I'll get them," said Becky.

Angie showed up, not wanting to miss an opportunity to visit with Glen.

Clinical Death

"Detective Karst, you owe me lunch. I picked up your dogs and made sure Mieke got bred."

"Make that two lunches," said Janet. "I'm the one who got the bad phone call with all that static and had to figure out what you were saying."

"It's a deal. I'll take you both to lunch on Saturday when I'm off duty."

"We're gonna hold you to it," said Angie.

"Not a problem. I'm good for it. How'd the surgery go?"

"Everything went fine, Glen. If all goes as expected, in nine weeks you'll be delivering a litter of puppies."

"Great, and Taffy?"

"She's one tough little dog. She's fine. She'll never make it through the metal detector at the airport with all of those screws in her body, but she should be fine. My guess is she'll develop a little arthritis in those areas as she gets older, but we'll worry about that later," said Janet.

Angie darted off to answer a phone call.

Glen pulled Janet aside. "What's this about another client biting the dust?"

"Sure is strange, isn't it? If this keeps up we won't have any clients left and we'll have to shut our doors. I guess I really shouldn't make light of this tragedy. What a terrible way to die. I heard he tried to eat the moldy corn at the bottom of the pit—nasty."

"Where's this guy live?" asked Glen.

"If you go south of your place about three miles and turn west another two, that'll take you to his farm. He has a small brick house and lots of outbuildings," said Janet.

"Where's who live?" asked Cal.

"Glen was just asking about Louis."

"Can you believe it? I've known Louis his whole life. What a shame. What a damn shame," said Cal.

"Have there always been so many farm tragedies in the county? I don't remember much growing up. I suppose my parents sheltered us kids from the bad things in life," said Glen.

"Farming comes with high risk. That's why it's difficult to get good health insurance at a fair price for farmers," said Cal.

Becky returned with Glen's dogs. She helped him load them then waved as he drove off.

He dropped the dogs off at home, then went further down the road to the Boyle farm to have a look at the crime scene. He thought he could do a little investigating without telling anyone.

The yard was filled with cars when Glen drove by. He slowed way down to get a good look at the layout of the farmyard. A quarter of a mile south of the main driveway

Clinical Death

he found a back entrance to the buildings. This must have been the access road Louis used with his machinery so as not to tear up the main driveway from the weight of the tractors and implements, especially on muddy days.

Glen pulled up to the Quonset huts on the backside of the farm. The crime scene tape showed him where the pit was located. He slipped under the tape then walked to the edge to peer down inside. The structure looked safe enough. A ladder allowed easy entry and exit through a hinged door on the top.

Glen studied the door. He thought to himself, if this guy would not have used a hinged system he may still be alive today. Had he lifted the door manhole style and slid it out of the way there would have been no way he could've become trapped.

He saw the irrigation pipes stacked in the building along the wall. Those must be the pipes that were on top of the door. He looked more closely the platform next to the door. A year's worth of dirt and debris had blown in around the pipes leaving behind the impression of the position of the pile. By the number of pipes and the number of empty places in the dirt, Glen calculated how wide the base was and how high he may have stacked them.

He wondered why anyone would be so careless as to loosely stack pipes next to a trap door in such a way with no braces to hold them back. He examined the two-inch pipe cattle panel wired to three upright wooden posts. Then he saw the rusty baling wire that must've secured the stack of pipes against the cattle panel.

He guessed the pipes were about twelve feet long with a circumference of about eight inches. It looked as though Louis wired them with the baling wire about every four feet. He looked at the first broken wire. Louis had bent and wrapped the wire around itself against the panel, weakening the wire at the twist. Glen remembered helping his dad and granddad fix fence. If you put too much twist on the wire it would snap in two. There were four strands of wire holding up the entire weight of all those pipes. Once again, he saw the break near the twist in the rusty wire.

"Why didn't he use nylon rope?" he said.

Glen, being thorough, checked the last two strands of wire even though he knew they would tell him the same story. To his surprise, they didn't. The last two strands of wire he examined were cut with a pair of wire cutters.

Glen placed his head in his hands and looked down toward the ground as he rubbed his forehead.

"Oh shit, not again. This is no accident it's a homicide, but what's the motive?"

Glen surmised someone cut those wires and probably pushed on the pipes. The weak rusty wire gave way sending them crashing over the top of the door, slamming it shut and resting on top.

Clinical Death

He got into his pickup to drive home. He wondered how to handle the knowledge he obtained at the crime scene. As he drove along the road he met Sheriff Tate's car about to pull into the main driveway to visit the widow. Glen waved him over.

"Evening, Sheriff."

"Glen, what brings you around here?"

"Guess you could say I was just being nosy. It's hard to stay away when accidents happen so close to home."

"That's exactly what it is, Glen. An accident. Don't go making something out of this like you tried to with Ed. I've already looked over the accident site and it's obvious Louis was down in the pit pounding away on the base of the ladder and the vibration must've caused the rusty wire to snap. Plain and simple, it was just an accident."

"So you took a good look at the wire holding the pipes?"

"I sure did," said Tate.

"Did you look at all four of them?"

"I said I looked at the wires, end of investigation, Detective Karst. Now if you don't mind, I'm going to go in and check on Rosemary."

Glen returned to his pickup knowing full well Tate had not checked each wire. Maybe to save face he'll go back and look later. Hopefully, he might make the discovery on his own and be a local hero. Somehow Glen doubted that would happen. He remained conflicted; the death of Louis deserved proper investigation. At the very least, he knew he must preserve the evidence he discovered.

Glen was anxious for a hot shower and bed. His exhaustion finally caught up to him. He'd been awake all night in the mountains then spent the day in the office wrapping up details on the Slater case. Coming back to discover another potential homicide near his home was more than he wanted to think about. He felt another migraine coming on.

He fed the dogs, poured a glass of bourbon and started the shower. After his shower he was too tired to cook so he grabbed a large handful of deli meat and some cheese, eating them without bread on his way to bed.

Early the next morning, his alarm sounded, bringing him back to a conscious state. A conscious state that also told him his migraine had worsened during the night. He could barely see across the room from a combination of pain and the rainbow, zigzag pattern blurring his vision.

He sat on the edge of the bed while his head throbbed incessantly. Weak, tired and with vision blurred he jumped up quickly, barely making it into the bathroom where he vomited from the sheer intensity of the pain. He reached for a bottle of migraine Excedrin only to find it empty.

Clinical Death

He slid onto the floor, resting his head on the cool porcelain of the bathtub. After a while he crawled to the kitchen where he had left his cell phone on the counter. He feared if he stood up the room would spin and cause him to vomit again.

He stayed on the floor while he called his office. He explained he might be late or not come in at all if he didn't feel better. He leaned his head back against the cabinet wondering how he would drive into town for some pain relief in the condition he was in. He should have known better than to go to bed with the migraine. His always gets worse during the night, but he was so tired he ignored it.

His phone rang. He was tempted not to answer. He looked at the caller I.D. and it was Jennifer.

"Jennifer, what's happening?" he tried to hide his pain.

"Glen, I thought I would call and see if your mountain search proved productive. I had a feeling you went back out after you took me home. When I didn't hear from you, I thought I'd call."

"You're right as usual. I found the body and the weapon."

"What's wrong? You don't sound like yourself."

"I'm not feeling well. I've got a migraine. I need to get to town to pick something up for it."

"You stay put. If you can wait until I get there, I'll help out."

"No, Jennifer. I really appreciate it, but I think I need to take some pain meds and go back to bed. I'm afraid I wouldn't be very good company."

"I did not say I wish for you to entertain me. I simply stated I'll be out to assist you. Give me less than an hour and I'll be there."

Glen slipped into a pair of sweats and climbed into his recliner with a blanket and a glass of bourbon. When he found himself in migraine hell he didn't care what time it was, bourbon took the edge off.

He hoped he would doze off, but no such luck. Time ticked away ever so slowly as he waited for Jennifer to arrive.

Finally, he heard a soft knock at the door. Before he rose up to answer, Jennifer let herself in. She went into the kitchen with the grocery bag she carried. When she returned Glen expected to see her with a glass of water and a pill.

He sat up only to find her empty-handed.

"How are you feeling?" she asked.

"Like hell."

"Are you up to sitting on the floor against the front of the sofa?"

Glen looked from her to the floor gauging his ability at the moment.

Clinical Death

Confused, he said, "Sure, I guess so."

"Okay, good. Then you slip onto the floor."

He obediently assumed the position on the floor while she moved the coffee table out of his way. She sat on the sofa directly behind him with one knee on each side of his shoulders.

Not wanting to wait any longer, Glen asked, "Did you bring something for my migraine?"

"Yes, I did. Please close your eyes and relax."

Oh hell, Glen thought to himself, some natural holistic shit and I'm suffering. He remained too polite to say anything and quickly changed his thoughts so Jennifer wouldn't read his mind. Even though she reassured him, he always felt vulnerable.

She placed her hands on both sides of his head. She gently positioned them then sat quietly.

After a few moments Glen squirmed a bit.

"Is there something wrong?" she asked.

"No. But whatever you're holding in your hands is getting pretty hot. Is it one of those gel-filled bags that heats up when you press the button?"

"Not exactly. Is the heat uncomfortable?"

"Not yet, but I don't want to see it get any warmer."

She rearranged her hands.

"How's that?"

"Better."

The two of them sat in silence for another fifteen minutes.

"How's the migraine?"

Glen knew he was still sleepy and the silence relaxed him. He thought about his migraine, a little at first then more intently.

"It's gone."

"Are you sure?"

He moved his head from beneath her hands. He blinked his eyes and rolled them around trying to bring back the pain. He moved his head from one side to the other then looked up and down. Finally, he shook his head back and forth.

"Son of a bitch, it's gone. How the hell did you do that?"

He turned around to see what she had used. Whatever it was, he wanted one for the medicine cabinet. To his surprise her hands were empty.

She smiled at the puzzled look on his face.

"Reiki. I used Reiki to relieve your migraine pain."

Glen stood up rubbing his head.

"What in the hell is Reiki?"

"It's an ancient method of transferring healing energy. Many cultures have used it for centuries. I'm a certified Reiki Master. Maybe someday you would like to learn it and become certified as well."

"How does it work?"

Clinical Death

"I use my body as a channel for the healing energy of the universe to come through to your body by way of my hands. I'm sure you've heard of others being healed by the laying on of hands. This is similar."

"Why did your hands get so hot?"

"The energy creates heat. Sometimes they get hotter than other times. Sometimes I feel a strong tingling and sometimes the person receiving the treatment can feel the tingle. It's quite fascinating, actually. I'll give you a book to read on the topic if you'd like. You can learn more about it from classes offered at healing arts centers around Denver and Fort Collins."

Glen remained confused. If someone had told him about this he's sure he wouldn't have been a believer. Now having experienced it, he had to believe, but he tried to convince himself it was nothing more than a coincidence.

Jennifer left him there to contemplate this new experience and returned with a large slice of cheesecake.

"I bought this for you as a reward for a job well done on locating that body."

"Now this I understand," he said as he took a bite of the cool, creamy dessert.

Chapter 10

Glen chose to attend Louis Boyle's funeral as a show of neighborly concern. His eyes scanned the group of people at the graveside service.

Rosemary and Louis Boyle had prospered in the farming community. Louis worked endlessly, rising before dawn and retiring late to bed. Rosemary, annoyed with his exhausting hours, tried to coax him to spend more time with her. Like so many other farmers, Louis needed a wife to cook and clean so he could spend his time working the soil, producing a crop to outshine the neighbor's. It became an obsession. No one seemed surprised when he killed himself working.

With no other family nearby, Sheriff Tate took it upon himself to comfort the widow. He sat with her in church for the service then escorted her to the graveside. He lost his wife to an accident when the brakes in her car failed on icy roads. Rosemary made an extra effort to cook and scheduled the other ladies to help clean for the sheriff while he mourned the loss of his wife.

Clinical Death

At the end of the service friends and neighbors offered their condolences. Glen fell in line with the others.

"Hello, Mrs. Boyle. My name is Glen Karst. I bought the old Watkins farm. I'm really sorry about your husband."

"Oh, yes, you're the detective I met at the vet clinic, aren't you?"

"Yes."

"Welcome to the community. I'm sure you're going to like it here."

"Thank you."

Glen decided this was not the time to explain he once lived here with his family. He knew the word would eventually spread as quickly as the fact that he is a detective.

Sheriff Tate extended his arm to Rosemary, escorting her to his car.

"He seems like a nice man," said Rosemary.

"I have my doubts," Tate replied. "He's a city homicide detective and he seems to think every death is suspicious," said Tate.

"Oh my, homicide. That's quite a job," she said.

"I'm glad you got to meet him. I don't want him coming to you trying to make a homicide out of Louis' death and getting you all shook up over nothing. Promise me if he tries to convince you it was anything other than an accident that you'll ignore him and tell me right away."

"I'm sure he's harmless."

"Please promise me."

"Okay, I promise," she said in a teasing voice.

Glen learned nothing from attending the funeral other than to familiarize himself with more faces.

The three vets were also present. Usually at least one of them represented the clinic at a client's funeral. When they returned to what began as a quiet morning at the clinic, a frantic woman ran in carrying her black Lab. The dog cried out in pain.

Immediately, the staff jumped into action. Maria led the client into an exam room. Janet and Cal donned their scrub tops and hurried in behind them.

"What happened?" asked Cal.

"She ran out into the street after a squirrel and got hit by a car. I saw the whole thing happen. Can you save her?"

Janet and Cal examined the dog, assessing her vitals.

"Maria, let's get some x-rays."

The owner wrung her hands and sobbed as she paced back and forth in the room. Janet left the room while Cal attended to the dog.

"Why don't you come with me?"

She took the owner into the back where she encouraged her to clean the blood from her hands and arms. She handed her a cup of coffee and sat with her.

Clinical Death

Cal joined them after examining the x-rays.

"There's been extensive damage to her hips. She's going to need surgery. Once we get inside we'll be able to tell if there's internal bleeding or organ damage."

"How much is this gonna cost? I just moved here and I don't have a job yet and I've got medical bills of my own."

"We're talking somewhere in the vicinity of a thousand dollars."

"A thousand dollars! I don't have that kind of money."

"We can arrange payments if you'd like," said Cal. "You know, if this happened in the city that bill could be three times as high."

"I love that dog but I really can't afford it. How long would she need care afterwards?"

"She'd have to stay with us for a while then we could let her go home to you but you're going to have to be there to help her go to the bathroom. She won't be walking for some time."

The woman burst into tears, "I can't, I just can't. Is she suffering?"

"She's in a lot of pain. We can give her something for that," said Janet.

"How much to put her to sleep? I don't want her to suffer."

Janet's heart went out to the woman. "I'll cover the expense if that's what you'd like to do."

"Thank you."

The young woman got up and rushed out of the clinic, not looking back at her dog. She couldn't bear to be there while the Lab was being put down. Susie and Becky cried as they watched her leave, sympathetic to her pain.

"What's going on?" asked Angie when she saw everyone crying.

"Oh, this lady has to put her dog down," sobbed Becky. "It was just too sad to watch her."

Angie hurried down the hall to the pharmacy. Maria had taken a syringe from the cabinet.

"Here let me. I know how much you hate this," said Angie.

"I can at least fill the syringe."

"No, that's okay. I really don't mind," insisted Angie.

She took the syringe from Maria then went to the cabinet for a small brown bottle to fill the syringe. She turned and called out to Maria, "How big is the dog?"

"Ninety-six pounds."

Maria stepped back into the room to speak to Angie.

"Wait, that's not the right drug. You have the wrong bottle."

Startled, Angie nearly dropped it.

"Really, Maria. I do this all the time, don't you think I'd know what I'm doing."

"I'm telling you that's the wrong bottle." She took it from Angie. "This is Ace Promazine. That's only a tranquilizer."

"Oh my God, you're right. I'm so stupid. Hey, what happened to this dog anyway?" asked Angie, in an attempt to draw Maria's attention away from the syringe.

"She's a black Lab that got hit by a car this morning."

"How bad?"

"Cal says she's gonna need surgery for her hips."

"Oops, that's my phone," said Angie.

"I didn't hear anything."

"I have it on vibrate." She glanced at her phone. "I really need to take this in private."

Maria stepped out of the room.

Angie pushed the speed dial on her phone to call Dr. Bradley.

"Is Dr. Bradley in, please?"

"She's with a client. Can I take a message?"

"Tell her this is Angie and it's important. I'll wait."

"Angie, what's up?" asked Allison Bradley.

"I have a female Lab, over ninety pounds with hip injuries from a car accident. The owner left her to be put down. Do you want me to bring her over?"

"Yes, but she can't wait until tonight. You'll have to do it right away. Make sure you sedate her first."

"That's my plan. I need to fake being sick or something so I can get out of here."

Angie stepped into the exam room with the syringe. Cal and Janet waited with the dog.

"I can take over from here," said Angie.

She sedated the dog and carried her out back, laying her body gently in the back of her pickup. With tinted windows on her topper, no one would know the dog was there.

She went back inside, holding her stomach as she walked to the front desk.

"Oh man. I feel like I've got the flu. I about puked my guts up out back. I've been running to the bathroom with diarrhea since I got here this morning."

She said it loud enough hoping one of the vets would hear her. It worked.

Janet said, "If you're sick get out of here before you make the rest of us sick. And stay home 'til you're feeling better."

Angie sped out of the parking lot and raced to Sterling watching for cops. If one stopped her, she'd explain she needed to take the dog in for emergency surgery to avoid a ticket. It worked last time.

Dr. Bradley and Angie worked for three hours on the Lab.

Clinical Death

"What do ya think?" asked Angie.

"The damage wasn't as bad as the x-rays you brought led me to believe. I'm expecting a full recovery. Good call."

"Do you think I should contact the owner to let her know her dog is okay?" asked Angie. "She took it pretty hard."

"I feel sorry for her, I really do, but we have too much to lose. Your job would be at stake and I'd probably lose my license. It's a breach of ethics to go against the wishes of the clients by saving all these dogs the way we do. Then Nancy and her mom would get in hot water and..."

"I know, I know. I get the picture. I know lots of dogs would die if we had to stop what we're doing."

"I'll call Nancy. I'm not sure how to handle the recovery on this one."

Dr. Bradley returned to the room.

"Nancy's out on a delivery in California. She won't be back for a while. This dog needs to be moved and she needs hospital care."

"Can Betty do it?"

"I'm sure she can. She's really good with the dogs but she can't pick her up."

"Dr. Bradley, you have a call."

She left the room. When she returned she said, "That was Betty. She said she'll come after the dog. She

177

just hired a new woman named Jean who can take care of the kennel while she and Nancy are gone."

"Great. I'm gonna head back to Wallace now before someone stops by to check on me."

"Hey, don't forget this Vizsla you're supposed to take back with you. My Aunt Eloise gave us some more money for our project. I bought some additional equipment so you can set up a makeshift hospital room. I'll help you load it."

***

Glen sat at his desk going through folders to find a new case to focus his attention on. He pulled out his notebook and began to write down facts about the deaths in Wallace. Once again, he had trouble keeping his mind off of those potential homicides.

He wondered how he could investigate the deaths without raising the suspicions of the already wary people of the town. He listed his two neighbors, Ed and Louis, and decided to add the name of Clyde Malcolm, the heart attack/drowning victim.

Bill joined Glen at his desk.

"Well, boss, where do we go from here? I still think you did one hell of a job with that Slater case even if you gave credit to your crackpot psychic friend. You knew from the get-go he did it. It was just a matter of time. You would've gotten him even without her help."

Clinical Death

Bill picked up one of Maggi Morgan's books from the rack on Glen's desk.

"You haven't mentioned Maggi in a while. Is she back in the area?"

"No, she's away writing a book of poetry to help her heal from everything that's she's been through."

"I guess she's never found her dogs, then?"

"Nope, that's part of why she needs a healing process."

"Since you help her with her books maybe you should just write one for her."

"If that isn't a stupid ass idea. Get off my desk and take half of these folders. Let's decide what we're doing next."

Bill walked away mumbling, "I still think you should write a book."

Glen shook his head as he closed his notebook containing the Wallace cases.

Wait a minute, he thought. That stupid idea might not be so stupid after all. If I can convince the community I'm writing some historical book about the area I bet they'll come out of the woodwork to talk to me. It just might work.

He finished the piles of paperwork needed to close the Slater case. The case now rests with the court system. He finished his part of the job; all that is left is to testify. His mind kept wandering to his book idea.

On the way home that evening he tossed around potential titles. He chose, *Farming, the Deadly Profession.* He could cut to the chase about investigating deaths without causing too much concern. He noticed the Wallace Library as he passed through town. He wanted to check their hours. He was in luck. They were open until eight Monday through Thursday. He went inside.

"Can I help you," came a voice from behind the desk.

Glen looked up into Cindy's face. As the library director she enjoyed greeting everyone who entered. Her smiling face and friendly voice made the patrons feel welcome.

"I'm doing some research for a book I'm writing and wanted to check out your library."

"Oh, you're a writer. How nice."

"Not really. I'm more of a wannabe writer. I'm really a cop, but I work with a writer on her books."

"Who is she? Maybe we have her books."

"Her name is Maggi Morgan."

"Oh my God, you work with Maggi Morgan? Are you Detective Karst?"

"How did you know that?"

"I love her writing. She mentions you in the credits of all her books."

"Gee, I thought no one ever read the credits."

Clinical Death

"When you admire a writer like Maggi Morgan, you read every word. So are you going to write your own murder mysteries?"

"No, I'm more into historical non-fiction. I'd like to spread my wings writing about Wallace and other nearby farming communities."

"You want to write the history of the area in general?"

"No, actually, I'd like to focus on the dangers of farming as a profession and how's it's changed over the years."

"That's a fascinating topic. I'm not sure anyone has ever done that before. You know we have a writer's group that meets here every Wednesday evening from six until eight. Would you like to join us?"

"That might be a good idea. Can you show me where you keep your newspapers or are you computerized now?"

"A little bit of both. There's a company that gets the papers from the newspaper office and puts them on microfilm for us. We have from 1904 up until 2004, so we're missing the last few years. But we do have the physical newspapers for that time period. I'll show you where to find them and how to run the microfilm machine."

"That would be great."

Glen followed Cindy as she led him toward the back of the library and into the smaller research room.

"How far back would you like to go?"

"I'm not sure yet if I want to go from the past to the present or from the present to past," he lied. He knew he wanted to find the most recent deaths and work his way back to identify a possible serial killer in Wallace.

Cindy showed him how to access the microfilm and where the newspapers are stored.

"Are you planning to work tonight or are you just wanting to learn the lay of the library?"

"I've got plenty of time to do research. I think I should go home and start my outline."

Glen had been around Maggi enough to understand much of the writing, printing and publishing world. He knew he had adequate knowledge to fake his way through this project. His main goal would be to convince the community he was truly writing a book.

"If I can be of any further assistance please ask. Oh, and if you talk to Maggi, tell her hello from one of her biggest fans."

"I'll do that," said Glen. "And thanks."

Cindy left the room. Glen looked up the most recent death to familiarize himself with the obituary section and learn how the local newspaper reports tragic accidents. He left the room as soon as he found what he was looking for since he told Cindy he wasn't ready for the research portion.

***

Dr. Bradley stayed late because she received a phone call from Betty, Nancy's mother, informing her that she was two hours away from Sterling. When she arrived, Dr. Bradley gave her a folder containing instructions on the care of the black Lab. She explained in great detail the amount and time to give pain relief along with feeding instructions and how to move her. She showed Betty how to use a brace to help the dog stand. She encouraged Betty to keep her as quiet as possible for the next few days using tranquilizers. Then, of course, there was the changing of the bandages and daily temperature.

"This is really a two-man job with a dog this size. Do you have someone there to help you until Nancy returns?"

"Yes, remember I told you I hired kennel help?"

"Yes, but you might need help around the clock."

"She'll be there. She's moved into the carriage house out back with her dogs."

"So what's her story?"

"It's a sad one. She's hiding from her ex-husband. He's a dangerous man. She fled from another state with her two Bernese Mountain Dogs and Jack Russell Terriers. Her name is Jean. She needed to board her dogs overnight and our vets suggested she use our facility. We got to talking and I offered her a job."

"Does she have any experience?"

"That's the best part. She used to run her own kennel and show dogs. She's a retired dog show judge. Her husband wanted to split the dogs in the divorce. She said he never liked them and wouldn't take good care of them. He just wanted to make her miserable worrying about them."

"Sounds like a perfect situation for you. How will you explain what we're doing?"

"That was pretty easy. She's accustomed to rescue kennels for purebred dogs. I told her we rescue any breed that needs a home and we match families with dogs."

"You didn't tell her the whole story, did you?"

"Give me more credit than that, of course not. I figured she's probably not telling me her whole story and as long as she's half the worker she appears to be, everything should be just fine."

"Are you ready to load this dog now?"

"Not really. I'd like to get a room and get some sleep. I'm not as young as Nancy and I don't have her stamina. I'd like to try to drive non-stop tomorrow with the dog sedated, if my body can handle it. So I want a full night's sleep before I start."

Clinical Death

"Okay, but you have to be here before my clinic opens at seven. I don't want any questions about you taking the dog."

"I'll see ya in the morning then."

***

Glen got up early Saturday morning to make a trip to Longmont to run errands. He planned to be back in Wallace by noon to honor his promise to Angie and Janet about their lunch date.

He took all three of his dogs with him. They were in the back of the pickup in the camper shell. As he approached the busy traffic area of Ken Pratt Boulevard, he wondered why this five-lane road would be so busy on a Saturday morning. Even the side roads had more traffic than usual. He noticed a little mop-looking dog had wandered out into traffic. He was unsure whether the dog had already been hit because it walked with a slight limp. He stopped his truck and tried to coax the little dog over to him. The dog responded to his kind voice and slinked toward Glen. He suddenly stopped when his owner and a gaggle of well-wishers ran toward him, calling his name. Glen saw what was about to happen. The dog turned and ran into traffic.

Glen jumped back into his truck and drove to the intersection. Thankfully traffic stopped and the little dog was unharmed. He edged his pickup to the side of the road as the little dog ran through a busy parking lot

185

heading back to Ken Pratt and the heaviest traffic. He let the two big girls out of the back of the truck. He pointed to the little mop of a dog and yelled, "Get the doggie!"

They quickly ran the dog down before he reached Pratt Blvd, grabbed him like prey and pinned him. Proud of his girls, Glen caught up to them.

Confident of his dogs' response, this seemed the best solution to a dangerous situation. Spectators were both surprised and amazed. They cheered as Glen picked up the little dog. Occupants of passing cars had stopped and they joined in the cheering. Finally, the owner reached them.

She was furious. She feared his dogs were attacking her little dog. Glen shook his head. The woman lacked the courtesy to even thank him.

As she walked away with her dog in tow, Glen said, "Maybe you should give your dog away. It says a lot about a person when your own dog won't even come to you."

She returned a nasty look.

Chapter 11

Angie and Janet were waiting in the front lobby for Glen to arrive for their lunch date. Janet knew he'd call if he couldn't make it. Phil's friend, Ron, from the Ogallala, Nebraska vet clinic, was in town for a visit. He spoke with Cal while Phil looked over bookwork.

"Hey, Janet. What's this write-off for Amy Sutton?" asked Phil. He kept his thumb on the financial aspect of the clinic more so than the other two vets.

"I don't recognize the name. What's it for?"

"Euthanizing a dog and some x-rays."

Ron looked up when he overheard the name.

"Oh, that," said Janet. "She was such a basket case having to put her dog down after a car hit it. She didn't have any money for surgery so I told her not to worry about the bill, I'd cover it."

"Amy Sutton?" asked Ron. "Was that a Lab?"

"Yeah, why?" asked Janet.

"I wondered what happened to her. She constantly came into our clinic with emergencies caused by her own

187

neglect. Then if she thought the price was too high, she'd have us put the dog down. She skipped out on her last two bills."

"You mean I've been had?" she asked.

"I'm afraid so. She raises Labs and lets them run loose all over the neighborhood. They've been in fights, hit by cars, shot at. You name it; we've seen it all with her. She fancies herself some big breeder of show and obedience Labs."

Just then Glen burst into the room, worried he was too late and the girls had given up on him.

"Well, it's about time. Someone could starve to death waiting on you," whined Angie.

"Gotta watch this one, Glen. She just got over a nasty case of the flu that took her away from work for two solid days. But she made it back today in time to go to lunch with you."

"Hey, if he's buyin', I'm eatin'. Let's go," said Angie.

Glen escorted the two ladies to his pickup. The three men followed them out the door.

"What the hell. I'm not buying for you thugs. Find your own free lunch. I don't need you guys around when I've got a date with two lovely ladies," said Glen.

"Don't get bent out shape, Glen, my boy. We have to work with these two all week. You're welcome to them. We'll make sure we eat at a different restaurant. Hell, we even might splurge and go to Burger King instead of McDonald's," laughed Cal.

During lunch, Glen explained his reason for being late. He told them the story of the little dog he saved from traffic.

"Yeah, right," said Angie. "I'll have to remember that one the next time I'm late for work."

"What's wrong with you?" Glen asked Janet.

"I guess I'm just a little distracted," she replied.

"Hey, is this a party and I'm not invited?" asked Sheriff Tate as he pulled up a chair.

Janet looked up, "Sit down, Tate, join us." She didn't care for the sheriff. What else could she do but be polite since he already invited himself. She felt he was too arrogant to be good company.

Glen read her expression and coupled with his own feelings for the sheriff, he thought, this should be amusing.

Glen appeared surprised that Tate would want to have lunch with him. He gave Glen the impression he disliked him.

"So what's got you so distracted?" asked Tate.

"She got scammed yesterday by a client," said Angie

Angie didn't feel the same way about him. He was single and she thought he might make a good catch.

"Oh yeah, who? Anybody I know?"

"I doubt it," said Janet.

"Amy Sutton. She moved into the old Phillips house outside of town," said Angie.

"Oh, the one with all those dogs?"

"That's her," said Janet.

Tate fancied himself a real ladies man. Janet's lack of interest annoyed him. He knew she was a married woman, but that shouldn't stop them from having a little fun.

He sidled up closer to Janet, putting his face near hers.

"What'd she do, make a play for your hubby?"

Janet sat back in her chair, pulling quickly away from him.

"She got Janet to foot the bill for her dog. She carried it into the clinic bleeding and in pain. Put on quite a show about how broke she was and how much she loved the dog. We put it to sleep. But we found out this morning she's done this to a lot of other vets. She lets her dogs run loose and they get hurt."

"I've already answered two calls about strays running along the road outside of town. Turned out they were her dogs. That's how I knew about her," said Tate.

Glen felt as though Tate ignored him on purpose. He sat back and observed the interaction between the three.

Clinical Death

Finally, he turned to Glen. "Karst, I trust you're not moonlighting in my jurisdiction."

"I'm keeping my nose where it belongs, if that's what you mean."

Tate stood up, pushed in his chair, tipped his hat to the ladies and left.

"Man, I'm glad I didn't mention my psychic friend to that asshole," mumbled Glen as Tate walk away.

"What psychic friend?" asked Angie.

"Jennifer Parker. My department uses her once in a while on a case."

"I thought all that shit was bogus," said Angie.

Janet shot her a nasty look.

"Well, isn't it?" she looked back at Janet.

"I used to think so, but I've seen her work. She's the real deal. She's helped us break a lot of cases," explained Glen.

They dropped the subject when the food arrived.

Amy Sutton spent the day working her Labs for the upcoming dog show. She missed Jackie, who had been euthanized. Amy had high hopes for finishing Jackie's third leg in the obedience trials in Denver. That night she went into town. She quickly became a familiar face at the local bar in Wallace. She liked to dance and they usually had a good disc jockey on Saturday nights.

She sat at a table near the window, hoping to meet someone new. The cars and pickups cruising main kept her attention. Dragging main has become a small town ritual. The bar closed at one o'clock. She stayed until the end. When she stepped outside to get into her car, she noticed a pickup that had been cruising earlier. She strained her eyes in the dark to see if it was a man or a woman driver. The combination of too many drinks and moonless night made it impossible for her to tell.

She waved as the pickup drove by, as is the friendly custom. As she drove along the empty street toward her house just outside of town, she noticed the pickup following her. She turned at the next corner and circled through town the back way to see if she was really being followed.

When she completed the circle and popped back out on the main street she found herself alone. She continued home. A mile further down the road where the paved street turned to gravel, she made a turn. The roads were void of streetlights. When she approached her driveway, she noticed something in the center of the road.

As her headlights shone ahead she saw one of her dogs had escaped and been hit.

"Oh no. Not again," she wailed.

She pulled over to the side of the road to check the body. When she got there, she realized it was a bundle of old clothes that someone had formed to look like an animal.

Clinical Death

"Who would have done such a thing?" she complained. "That could be dangerous. Someone could swerve at the last minute and have an accident."

As she bent down to remove it headlights from a vehicle parked down the road flashed on, blinding her. Shielding her eyes she tried to determine who or what it was.

The engine revved then the vehicle sped toward her so quickly she had no time to react. In a split second, Amy lay crumpled on the road as the vehicle raced away.

The next day being Sunday, Glen decided to go for a walk down the road with his dogs. He wanted to see how well Taffy handled the distance with her delicate leg. The advantage of her being a small dog is he could carry her back if she showed signs of discomfort. He only planned to walk about a quarter of a mile, but the dogs were having such a good time digging up mice in the ditches and smelling the scents of the animals of the night.

They reached the property line between his and Ed's place. Mieke first then Cheyenne pricked their ears. Little Taffy, with her big ears, heard the same whining sound as the big dogs. She started down the ditch and up the other side, slipping under the barbed wire fence so quickly Glen worried about her leg.

"Taffy," he called.

She kept running.

"Damn it. Taffy, come back here."

The little dog disappeared in the brush, totally out of sight.

Glen looked at his other two dogs who stayed obediently at his side.

"Well, don't just stand there. Go get her."

Joy filled their bodies and they bounded down the ditch, hot on the trail of the little brown dog. Glen followed as they quickly pulled away from him. Finally, when he reached the other side of the barbed wire fence and flatter ground, he could see all three dogs circling around the barn where he had found the Australian Shepherd and her companion.

They must smell where those other dogs had been. Then he heard the sound of a dog from inside the barn. He gave his dogs the stay command. The big dogs obeyed, but little Taffy tried to squeeze into the barn between Glen's legs. She yelped as he tried to scoot her back, bumping her sore leg. He realized she pushed too hard on her run.

He discovered someone had gone to a great deal of trouble to improve the living conditions of the dogs kept there. He found a stainless steel stack of four crates resembling those in a vet clinic. Inside one of the large cages he saw a Vizsla. Her belly had been shaved, indicating a recent surgery.

Clinical Death

I bet that's why the conditions are more sterile. This big...he looked under the dog, girl, must've been through some surgical procedure. He examined the cage and surroundings. She had plenty of food and fresh water. The bars on the cage floor allowed the urine and feces to drain through so the dog would not come in contact with her own excrement.

On a table nearby he found bottles of antibiotics and painkillers. Whoever was responsible for caring for these dogs obviously knew what to do.

Mieke's bark caught Glen's attention. He climbed the stall rails to look out the window. He couldn't see much through the dirty windows covered with over-spray from painting the barn. He jumped down. Opening the heavy doors he dashed out to gain a better view of the driveway.

Someone had come to care for the dog. Glen's dogs must've been in clear view causing whomever it was to leave in a hurry before Glen could make out the color or type of vehicle. All he saw was a cloud of dust and he heard the spray of gravel. He knew by the time he ran to the bottom of the driveway the vehicle would be over the hill, totally out of sight.

Glen looked at his watch. He wanted to gauge the time the caretaker made rounds. He planned to come back without his dogs. He could easily hide in the hayloft and wait for the unsuspecting mystery person to return.

He still didn't understand why it bothered him so much. It really was none of his business. He tried to convince himself to let it go, but the detective in him needed answers.

He closed the barn door, scooped up Taffy and called to the other dogs. They walked back by way of the road. They met no passing cars or trucks. He thought about going back to check the tire pattern in the soft soil, but talked himself out of it.

He knew the task of sorting through the deaths around the county should be enough to keep him busy without adding the mystery of the disappearing dog act.

He entered the den and went to his desk. He opened the top drawer and pulled out a yellow legal pad and pen. He sat on the porch swing and began his outline and notes to fake his way through the writer's class. He needed the local gossip to make his book credible.

**

Bill brought his notes to Glen's desk.

"What's this?"

"We have a robbery homicide case to close."

"Tell me about it."

Bill opened the folder.

"Seems this jerk burst into a convenience store, raped the clerk then blew her away along with two customers who walked in on him. He cleared the register and loaded up with all the cigarettes and beer he could carry."

Glen looked at the blurry black and white photo printed from the film of the surveillance camera.

"Is this it?" he asked as he thumbed through the folder.

"Yep."

"No witnesses?"

"Dead."

"Surely someone heard the gunshots and can give us a description of the car. There has to be something to go on."

"I'm sure there is," said Bill. "But it's up to us to find it. There's reason to believe he's on a roll. Two other stores in the past six months have had the same M.O. Sarge wants us to stop him before he hits again."

Glen and Bill took down the addresses of the three stores, then went out to beat the bushes for witnesses. Even if they found someone who had been present during the time of the robbery and rapes, getting them to testify or even talk to the police could be difficult. Even then their information could be inaccurate.

Exhausted after a day of walking the streets, knocking on doors and talking to strangers, Glen found they were no further into the investigation than when they started.

He rubbed the back of his neck as he drove through Wallace on his way home past the library. Suddenly, he had a new burst of energy. He drove around the block to park in front of the building. He shuffled through the paperwork on the seat until he found the yellow legal pad with his book outline scribbled across the first few pages.

He allowed a number of lines between his notes, just as he had seen Maggi do, so he could add more. He flipped rapidly through the pages.

"Not bad. I think it looks legit," he said. He checked his watch. He still had two hours before the library closed.

The computer stations were full. There were two librarians behind the counter. An older couple sat at a table reading the newspaper. The smell of old books, old wood and old carpet reminded him of how aged and rustic this library was. How strange to look around at the walls that probably had not seen fresh paint for years, only to notice the brand new computer area. Near the computer desks stood shelves of audio books and DVDs—how well the old blended in with the new.

Glen made his way through the cases of books to the small room that containing the microfilm. He reached for the doorknob and his cell phone vibrated in his pocket. He quickly threw the door open and closed himself in the room. He recognized Bill's number on the caller I.D.

Clinical Death

"What's up?" he whispered.

"Why are you whispering?"

"I'm in the library. What do you want?"

"I thought maybe we should meet at the convenience store instead of driving all the way to the office. Might shave some time off tomorrow."

"Sure, great. What time?" asked Glen.

"How about eight thirty?"

"Okay, see ya there."

"Wait. What're you doing in the library?"

"Reading," said Glen as he hung up the phone.

Downstairs Cindy turned off her office light. Another late night did not seem out of the ordinary. She worked more late nights than she'd like, but at the moment, her social life wasn't booming.

"Good night," she told her workers.

"It's about time you got out of here," replied Pam.

Pam, an older woman about ready to retire, had been at the library for over twenty years. She enjoyed meeting new people and introducing children to the magic of books.

"Looks like business as usual," said Cindy as she peered around the library.

"Almost," said Pam. "That handsome detective you were talking to last week is in doing research for that book you said he planned to write."

Cindy turned to catch a glimpse of the door hiding the detective from her vision.

"I wondered how serious he was," she said. "Now I know. I think I'll pop my head in and see if he needs anything before I leave."

"Good idea," said Pam with a sparkle in her eye. Her other favorite pastime was playing matchmaker.

Cindy quietly opened the door.

"Good evening, Detective Karst."

Glen looked up from the papers he had opened on the table in front of him.

"Please, call me Glen. No need for that detective stuff. Glen's fine."

She slipped into the room.

"Am I interrupting?"

"Nope."

She noticed the dates on the newspapers.

"I see you decided to begin from the present and work your way back."

"Gotta start somewhere."

Cindy glanced down at his notes on the yellow paper.

"Looks like you're serious about this book."

"Absolutely. When I set my mind to something I always follow through."

"I'm sure that's what being a detective is all about."

Clinical Death

Glen looked through the paper trying to find the story about Ed's death.

"Is there something I can help you find?"

"I was looking for Ed Kurtleman's obit and story."

"If you're starting at the present, don't you want Louis Boyle first?"

"That's true. Let's start there."

Cindy took that as an invitation to stay. She set down her handbag and began thumbing through the stacks of papers.

"You did want only deaths that are farm-related, not other accidents, right?"

"No, I'd like all accidents."

"I'm not sure how they would tie into your topic of farming being such a deadly profession."

"I'd like to have all the facts in case I change my storyline along the way. No sense in having to do double the research. I'll list them separately, though."

"I don't suppose you want the death that happened Saturday night?"

"What death?"

"It wasn't farm-related. I suppose you could call it an accident."

"Who died?"

"Some new person in town. Well, actually she moved here about the time you did. Her name was Amy something or other."

"Amy Sutton?" asked Glen.

"Yes, I believe that was her last name. Do you know her?"

"No, I've never met her. I overheard some people talking about her."

Glen, as always, remained guarded about the source and amount of information he gave out freely.

"It didn't take you long to become part of the gossip ring."

"It's all part of my job keeping my eyes and ears open. I'm pretty good with faces and names."

Glen reached for his pen. He picked up his pad preparing to take notes.

"Tell me what happened to Ms. Amy Sutton."

"I don't know much, other than what I heard through the gossip. The story will be out in the paper on Wednesday I'm sure. Of course, you can always go talk to Sheriff Tate about it. I'm sure he can give you more details than I can."

"That's a good idea, but why don't we start with what you know."

For a town that loved gossip, it quickly became apparent that Cindy must be a transplant as hard as he had to work to pull the story from her.

"Amy lives alone just outside of town. Last night she was at the bar until closing time. Talk is she left there drunk, but you didn't hear that from me. Anyway, she drove home and, for some reason, tried to walk across the road away from her house instead of toward it. It was very dark last night and someone must've flown up over the hill on their way into town and hit her. They must've thought they hit a deer because they never stopped to see if she was okay."

"A hit-and-run?"

"Yeah, a hit-and-run."

"Who found her?"

"Sheriff Tate. He was out on patrol last night looking for kids that had been out partying on Saturday night."

"Does he have any leads?"

"Not from what I heard. He's guessing it was some teenager heading back into town."

"So he thinks it was a town kid?"

"Apparently."

Glen started a new page. He charted it like he would at work. He created a column for the name of the victim, another for the date and time. Then he added one for the place, cause of death and the witnesses or person responsible for finding the body.

"Is that the way you do it at work?" asked Cindy as she watched over his shoulder.

"Actually, it is. Normally, I'd be writing it on white board. See how everything falls nicely into the columns.

When we're working on multiple homicides or a serial killer it helps us to see patterns develop.

"We can tell if he strikes on a certain day of the week, if he only kills women or if he likes a certain neighborhood or time of day. As the list grows, the more information we have, the tighter we can draw connections and often predict when and where he might hit again."

"So, if this were a real investigation, right now Sheriff Tate would be a suspect then?" asked Cindy.

Glen looked back at his notes.

"I'd say, at this point, with no other names on the chart, in this investigation Sheriff Tate would be our only suspect."

Chapter 12

The news media incited fear in the residents of Denver with the story of a crazed serial killer on the loose. Many times during a crime investigation, circumstantial evidence might link two cases together before the authorities can prove otherwise. If the media presented all crime in this manner, the citizens of Denver would either live in constant fear or become negligent.

On day three of the investigation no leads surfaced. They both knew this case would be long and drawn out. The general public has no idea the amount of grunt work behind the scenes: several hours of questioning people, footwork walking to each business inquiring about frequent customers who may have witnessed the event, anything to simplify their jobs.

Glen felt his attention divided. Normally, he'd put all of his energy into catching the bastard who raped and killed the female clerks but the happenings in his own backyard split his focus. How could Sheriff Tate be so nonchalant concerning the death of Amy Sutton? He couldn't avoid a proper investigation by ruling it another farm accident. Someone ran the poor woman down. Foremost in Glen's mind was to determine whether it was intentional or accidental. He felt Tate might present a strong case for the deer scenario. Accidents involving deer along country roads at night were a common occurrence.

"I'm outta here," said Bill. "See ya tomorrow."

Glen glanced at the clock on the wall, a bad habit he avoided. His work ethic forced him to continue until he was either exhausted or finished. However, tonight would be different. He planned to bluff his way through his first writer's meeting.

When he walked into the library, Pam led him downstairs to a table lined with strangers chattering about their latest attempts at writing. Silence fell over the group. He quickly noticed he was the only man present.

Cindy approached Glen.

"You didn't tell me this was a ladies only group," he whispered.

"It's not. We have men here occasionally. Tonight is just not one of those nights. Please, come in and join us.

"Ladies, we have a real treat tonight. This is Detective Glen Karst. He'll be joining our little group. That is, if we make him feel welcome."

Sandy, a mother in her early thirties with short blond hair, popped up, "I guess my suspense writing won't hold a candle to yours. You've got real life experience to write about."

"Actually, Glen's writing a historical book. No, I guess that's not the best way to describe it. Glen's writing a book about...well, you tell them, Glen."

Glen pulled up a chair.

"Oh, one more thing before Glen takes the floor. I have to add that this Detective Glen Karst is the one and only Detective Glen Karst who acts as a consultant for Maggi Morgan."

"Whoa," said Donna, a retired schoolteacher. "Does that mean we can use you for a consultant and make millions from our books like Maggi Morgan does?"

"I can't guarantee that," laughed Glen. "I think Maggi's writing talent has more to do with making her millions than my consulting."

"Tell us about your book," said Marcy, the youngest of the group.

"I'm writing about the dangers of farming as a profession. I'm sure all of you ladies will probably be able to help me more than I can help you," he said humbly.

"Are you wanting to know about accidents or deaths?" asked Donna.

"Mostly deaths."

"Do you want animal deaths or people deaths?" asked Marcy.

"I guess if the animal died from a farm-related injury, I'd like to know about it," said Glen, hoping to distract them from his focus on human fatalities.

"Speaking of deaths, did you all read about that Amy woman in today's paper?" asked Sandy.

Glen's ears perked up. This might be a great place to get insider gossip. Later, he could sort fact from fiction, but most often there's a spark of truth in gossip.

The discussion was a bust, as Glen didn't glean any useful knowledge. The only thing he learned was Tate's car had been seen at Amy's house on several occasions in the evenings. But Tate had previously mentioned he'd been called about her dogs multiple times, using those visits as a ploy to get closer to her. Glen chose to tuck that piece of information away for further use.

When he fed his dogs that night he noticed Mieke didn't finish her supper and Cheyenne was more than happy to help her. It was late, so he chose not to call the clinic and get someone out of bed simply because his dog skipped a meal. It could wait until the next day.

In the morning, the dogs accompanied him for a good run down the road. He ran while his dogs had more freedom to explore. He was always aware of the leg injuries on two of the dogs. He jogged in the mornings whenever he could fit it into his schedule. He appreciated not having to inhale exhaust fumes as he ran in the country with no traffic.

He took a hot shower, grabbed a quick bite then fed the dogs. Again, Mieke picked at her food and, once again, Cheyenne wolfed down the excess.

Glen called Bill.

"Hey, I'm gonna be about an hour late this morning. Do you want me to meet you at the office or the diner next to the convenience store? I'm gonna stop by the vet on my way through town."

"Something wrong with your dogs?"

"I don't think so, but I want to talk to one of the vets about Mieke's lack of appetite."

"Okay, let's meet at the diner."

Glen put the dogs out back then left. As he drove into the clinic parking lot he noticed he arrived before the veterinarians. He stepped in the front door hoping to slip out quickly if the vets were gone. The techs and the office help really liked to corner him to talk when the vets were away.

"Where is everybody?" he asked when he spotted Becky.

"Let's see..." She opened the appointment book.

"They wanted to get an early start at Larry Swanson's working cattle. They should be here in about an hour."

"Thanks, but I need to get to work," said Glen.

"You'll drive right by the Swanson place on your way to Denver. Let me give you directions."

Becky drew a map for Glen. She loved being the one who could assist him.

"Thanks," said Glen. "You're a peach."

He pulled into the farmyard along side of the other pickups. It seems nearly everyone in the county owns a truck. He followed the sound of cattle making a ruckus, annoyed at being handled by humans. They were content to be fed, watered and left alone. Particularly during occasions like this, where they were sorted, pushed and shoved into pens or squeeze chutes for vaccinations and other procedures.

Angie waved when she saw Glen. Phil and Cal looked up to see who she waved at. They nodded their heads toward Glen. His eyes scanned the dusty corrals for Janet. He found her sitting on a fence, working the gate allowing only one cow into the pen at a time.

Glen joined her on the fence. Years had passed since he worked cattle as a boy; the sounds and smells brought back many memories, as did the choking dust.

"Is there a problem?" she asked, trying to speak over the bellowing of the cattle.

"It's Mieke. She's not eating."

"That's probably a good sign. I'd say she's pregnant. Keep an eye on her though. We don't want her to pick for too many days—maybe one or two. If it goes on beyond that let's give her something to settle her stomach. Has she been vomiting?"

"Nope, I've been watching for that."

"Some dogs do for day or two until their hormones settle down. Just watch her."

"Thanks, I need to get to work now. Don't have too much fun." He tried to laugh, but choked instead on the dust and manure floating in the air.

Sheriff Tate appeared on the scene as Glen was about to leave. The men decided to take a break. Glen wanted to hear what he had to say but didn't want to seem obvious. He took his cell phone out and pretended he had a call. He put his finger in one ear as if to drown out the noise.

"Hey, Larry. Did you mean to hang your dog?" asked Tate.

Everyone gathered around to hear what he was talking about.

"What happened to my dog?" asked Larry.

"I just came from the house and saw your dog hanging over the fence. I cut him down."

Maria and Angie exchanged glances, trying to figure out if Tate was serious or not.

"You're not serious, are you? I tied him up this morning to keep him out from under foot. He can really screw things up when we're trying to work cattle in pens."

The entire group followed Tate to the yard where he laid the body of the Irish Setter under the tree near the fence where he'd been tied.

Glen followed at a distance. He observed the scene as he drove away.

"Geez, Larry. Didn't you know any better than to tie a dog so close to a fence?" scolded Janet.

"Apparently not," said Angie.

Phil squatted down to examine the dog to be certain he was dead and not just passed out.

"He's gone. Sorry, Larry."

Janet looked at her watch.

"It's getting late. I'll take the girls back to the clinic with me. You two finish up. There's about twenty head left to vaccinate."

Janet and the girls stomped away.

"Whew, she's pissed," said Cal. "Women. Sometimes they don't accept the real world too well."

"What was Karst doing here?" asked Tate. "Don't tell me he's investigating the death of one of your herd. Could be a homicide, ya know?"

The other men failed to show appreciation for Tate's humor about Glen. The others liked and respected him.

"He had a question about his dog, that's all," said Phil.

Clinical Death

"Why don't you back off and cut him some slack?" said Cal. "I've known Glen since he was a boy. He's a good guy. I'd do anything in the world for him. You should be pleased to have him as part of this community. If your sorry ass was on the line with a real criminal, you'd be damn lucky to have Glen at your side. He's gotten awards for being a sharpshooter ya know and he's an expert in hand-to-hand combat."

"No, I didn't know," said Tate with disgust in his voice. "I don't need no city dick covering my ass. I'm capable of taking care of myself. Don't forget I had to qualify, same as him," he said as he patted his gun.

"Did you stop by for any reason?" asked Larry, attempting to change the subject.

"Nah, I was out driving around and saw the bunch of trucks in your yard and wondered if something was wrong. So I pulled in to check. I've got to get back to town."

He turned to walk away.

"Arrogant little bastard," said Cal under his breath.

Glen received a call on his way to meet Bill.

"Good news. We may have something," said Bill.

"What?"

"Our guy hit again early this morning. This time the woman wasn't alone. Her boss was in the back sleeping. He decided he didn't want his lady clerks alone during the night shift. He heard her scream and came out with a gun. The perp saw him and fled the scene. The owner got off a couple shots and hit him. He must've grabbed his arm. He got blood on his good hand and left some great prints on the doorframe and handle. Hopefully, the son of a bitch is in the system and we can nail him."

"Outstanding! He may have solved the case for us. I wish more owners would be so careful with their female clerks when things like this are happening—might put a stop to it," said Glen.

Together they waited at Glen's desk for the report on the prints. If Bill wanted to visit with Glen at the department he learned early on that Glen couldn't tolerate being near Bill's desk. It was always littered with tipped over coffee cups, papers spread across the desk, jelly napkins and old pizza slices mixed among the papers. It was a wonder Bill could get anything accomplished. Aside from his rude behavior and nasty hygiene, Bill had strong instincts surpassing most other cops. If Glen tried to explain to him that he might have some psychic abilities responsible for those instincts, Bill would ask to switch partners immediately.

They got the call—a ten-point match to Curt Tobin. He'd been arrested previously on sexual assault charges, always managing to get off by threatening the victims. Following that, he chose to kill his witnesses. The mug shot on Glen's computer screen revealing a close enough match to the bad photo from the surveillance camera, combined with the prints, convinced them they had their man.

He wrote the affidavit to get the warrant. Most of the judges knew Glen well from past warrants and trials so when they noticed him standing at the back of their courtrooms, they often stopped their proceedings and summoned him up front immediately. Glen's secret was going to the civil court judges—they were eager to stop the mindless bickering in their courtrooms to issue an important warrant.

Glen pulled Tobin's last known address from the computer intelligence files and they went off to find him. One of the narcotics officers, a friend of Glen's, volunteered to watch the apartment for activity until Glen and the SWAT team arrived. Having been a past member of the team, he gained the respect and credibility he needed with them to work well together. They knew if Glen had already scouted out the area he made their job easier.

Within the previous hour Glen had changed clothes and taken his truck to the rundown Crown Regency Hotel in downtown Denver. He posted magnetic signs on his doors and with his clipboard and tape measure appeared nothing more than another contractor hired by the owner of the drug-infested hotel.

He quickly learned everything he needed to know about the perp's apartment: door, locks, escape routes, layout, human traffic in and out and lastly, the likelihood that Tobin was inside.

Glen and Bill had been on many drug busts at this same hotel.

The smell of meth was in the air as they stepped up to Tobin's door.

"Look here," said Bill.

Glen looked at the door. Blood from Tobin's wound told them he'd returned after the attempted robbery this morning.

Bill knocked at the door—no answer. SWAT waited everywhere and nowhere for Glen's signal.

The unlocked door swung open when Glen pounded harder. They had a clear view of the living room from the entrance. Tobin lay motionless on the floor. SWAT rushed in to clear the apartment.

They found Tobin passed out from the loss of blood. Bill applied a tourniquet to his arm while Glen called for an ambulance.

A moaning Tobin opened his eyes. He attempted to pull away from the detectives. Bill twisted his arms painfully behind him and cuffed him. He leaned him against the sofa while they waited for the paramedics.

Clinical Death

The paramedics arrived, attended to Tobin's arm then took him downtown to the hospital for treatment before the cops took him to his cell.

"I wish they were all this easy," said Glen.

He and Bill returned to the department to fill out the mountain of paperwork to accompany this case. Once again at five sharp Bill left for the day. Glen wondered why he kept such a tight schedule; he had no wife or family to go home to. Hell, he didn't even own a dog.

Glen hurried home to feed his dogs. Tonight Mieke gulped her food making Glen feel relieved. He changed his clothes then headed off to the library to continue the research for his bogus book. Mieke would not leave his side so he took her along.

Tonight Cindy was waiting for Glen. She learned enough about him to know he'd be stopping by on a regular basis until he'd exhausted his use of the library.

When Glen opened the door to the research room he found Cindy with a thermos of hot coffee and a home-baked streusel coffee cake. She had already started going through the papers where they'd left off.

"Cindy, what a pleasant surprise. What's this?" he asked when he saw the coffee and cake.

"I don't know about you, but I got hungry the other night when we worked so I thought tonight I'd bring snacks."

"That's really great. I appreciate it. Does this mean you're my research buddy?"

"If you think you need one. I'm available."

"What's your husband think about that?"

"Don't have one."

"And your kids?"

"Grown and gone."

"Dog?"

"Nope, a cat."

"Okay, then let's work." He pulled up a chair.

She sliced the cake and poured two cups of coffee.

"Where'd we leave off?" he asked.

"Before we get started, I thought I'd better you know I did a little detective work on my own."

"Awesome," said Glen. "What'd you find out?"

He took a bite of the cake.

"Wow, great cake," he said with his mouth full.

"Thanks, I like to cook," said Cindy. "Today I called the local mortuaries to ask how many deaths are in this county in a year's time."

"What'd you learn?"

"One said about a hundred and thirty and the other said about a hundred and forty. So I thought that was pretty normal. Then I called a few other counties about the same size. Their answer was a little lower but pretty close."

"I'm not sure what you're getting at," said Glen.

Clinical Death

"I pushed a little more on the phone and found out that not only does Wallace county seem to have more deaths, but more accidental farming deaths."

"But that's only by a small margin. Not really significant. There always has to be one county that has the most, it just happens to be ours," said Glen.

"I know, I thought the same thing, but as I pushed with my questions I found out that the primary cause is imminent death of the sick and elderly in all of the other counties, followed by car accidents. But here, in Wallace, there seems to be more accidental deaths of people from ages twenty to sixty who were in good health."

"Those facts or hearsay?" asked Glen.

"I can't answer that for you. I really don't know—could be nothing more than gossip."

"Hey, you might have something there. It's just that we need to find the actual facts to qualify the statement. Now you're gonna learn what being a detective is all about, tons of work that nobody knows about or gives a shit about. The public's only interest lies in the outcome of the case, not what you had to do to get there. Makes my job a little less glamorous when you're actually doing it."

"I guess once we've gone through the papers for the past forty or fifty years you might have the statistics you need to prove my theory."

"Exactly," said Glen. "Exactly."

Cindy helped Glen until closing time. Together they sifted through the stories in the papers. When they found one they needed Cindy made a copy. Soon Glen had a small stack accumulating, telling the sad tale of the deaths in Wallace, Colorado.

Reading through articles on more than one hundred deaths in a year made the forty-year target a long way from completion.

"Would you like to continue tomorrow night?" asked Cindy. "Or do you have to get home to your wife and kids?"

"No wife, no kids, but three dogs. Let's take a break tomorrow night. I'd like to read over what I've got so far."

Glen walked Cindy to her car.

"Are you doing anything Saturday night?" he asked.

"Why no, did you want to work again? The library's closed on Saturday nights."

"I know. I also like to cook and I thought I'd fix you supper for all the help you've been giving me. If you don't mind eating with a bachelor cop and his three dogs out on a lonely, old farm."

"I'd love it. Give me directions and tell me what time."

Clinical Death

Glen scribbled the directions onto the back of one of the sheets Cindy had copied for him along with his phone number.

"Now remember, I need that paper so you have to show up."

"It's a deal. See you Saturday."

Saturday morning Glen slipped away leaving his dogs in the yard. He took the back way through the pastures to Ed's farm. He searched the area for any signs of the vehicle that sped away last weekend at this same time of the morning.

He quietly darted across the barnyard using cover and concealment SWAT-style. As he opened the door the Vizsla alarm sounded. She stood up in the cage wagging her tail and barking excitedly at Glen. He had the opportunity to exam her belly. The stitches had been removed and she was healing nicely.

He climbed the stairs to the hayloft to take his position for the stakeout. He leaned back against the old straw bales. He watched the sparrows and barn swallows fly in and out of a broken window, building their nests. His eyes wandered along the walls and rafters as his mind took him back to the hours he and his siblings spent playing in their hayloft.

He recognized the hooks, pulleys and forks they used to move the hay. He saw old horse hames and collars speckled white from bird droppings. He estimated the barn to be around one hundred years old. He marveled at how well the floor of the loft held up after so many years.

He watched a spider respond to the motion in her web when a fly landed. She scurried to the fly, sucking the life juice from its body then discarding it to join the pile of others on the floor beneath the web.

City people have no idea of the society of life within the walls of an old barn. As he sat perfectly still he watched a small mouse check out the pile of dead flies then scurry off to the straw in search of full wheat heads to nibble for breakfast. He was sure the mice loved the dog food dropped and left behind by the visiting canines.

Glen heard the sound of a vehicle approaching. Tempted to rise up and look out of the window he declined, not wanting to take a chance of being seen. He dropped to his belly and crawled carefully across the floor to a spot where he could peer across the barn to the stall that housed the dog.

Again the Vizsla sounded her alarm as the door opened. He watched as the figure stepped inside, leaving the door open allowing a beam of sunlight to shine in.

"And how are you doing today?"

Glen tried to shuffle forward for a better look.

"What's that?"

His mystery person turned at the sound of Glen's body moving upstairs in the loft.

Clinical Death

"Are you hiding a cat in here?"

Glen closed his eyes to listen to the voice of a woman. A voice that sounded familiar.

She spoke again.

He recognized the sound of Angie's voice.

She finally walked into a position where he could see her clearly.

The mystery was solved. It was Angie who was taking care of the dogs. It must've been Angie who kept the dogs at his place. Angie and her big heart refused to let them be destroyed because they had bad owners.

Now he had the answer. What would he do with it?

Chapter 13

Cindy arrived at Glen's house with a bottle of wine and the leftover coffee cake. He gave her a quick tour of the house and buildings. Cindy preferred living in town, but could understand a single guy and his dogs would find it a peaceful retreat.

"Here's your paper from the other night," she said, still clutching it in her hand. The directions Glen scribbled on the back made it easy to find her way.

"Great. Just put it in my office with the others."

"Can I help you with anything?" she asked when she joined him in the kitchen.

"Nope. I've got everything under control. Go ahead and make yourself comfortable at the table, the food will be ready soon."

Glen opened the bottle of wine, took two glasses from the cabinet and poured. He set his wine glass next to his half full glass of bourbon.

""Ummm, everything smells so good. What're you fixing?"

Clinical Death

"Beef short ribs with cornmeal dumplings," he said. "I smoked some ribs, fried some bacon, roasted some garlic and onion and blackened some tomatoes then I threw it a pot with some beer and bourbon and voila', heaven."

"Wow. I'm impressed. I have to admit I assumed we'd be having steaks on the grill and baked potatoes. I don't know many men who like to spend time in the kitchen."

Glen chuckled, "I don't. Spend time in the kitchen that is. This is only the third meal I've cooked since I got here. With my schedule, it's easier to grab a meal in Denver or throw something together here. Some nights I eat a bowl of cereal or peanut butter and crackers. I only really cook for company, but I enjoy it."

As the evening progressed, they laughed and discussed their lives before Wallace. Glen's instincts were correct. Cindy was a local; she moved here about one year before Glen.

"What do you think of small town living?" he asked.

"It takes a little getting used to. I'm not accustomed to having my every move watched and talked about. I'm sure if you lived in town and someone saw my car parked here it would be all over town before breakfast tomorrow."

"Even though I live this far out someone will know you're here. Is that a problem? Should we have parked your car inside one of my barns?"

"Heavens no. I really don't care," she said.

Cindy helped Glen clear the table but he refused to allow her to help with the dishes. They stacked them in the sink and went into the living room to finish their wine and conversation.

"I brought you something," she said. She went to the sofa to remove papers from her purse, handing them to Glen.

"What's this?" he asked as he unfolded them.

"When you didn't show up last night I continued to go through the newspapers. This is a new stack. I'm afraid I didn't get very far. I made it from January until October. I really wanted to finish the entire year, but the library closed."

"Thanks, but you didn't have to do that. I feel bad."

"Don't. It's a fun project. Besides, it'll help me learn more about Wallace. I think it takes me so long because the headlines about local events catch my eye and I scan them for content."

Glen set down his drink to look through the sheets.

"I planned to go through the others last night, but it never happened," he told her.

Clinical Death

"Do you want me to help you sort them now?"

"I couldn't ask you to do that. You've done so much already."

"I told you I don't mind. Maybe you'll mention me in your credits."

"Credits? Oh yeah, the book."

"Of course, the book. What else did you think I meant?"

"I'm sorry, I was distracted reading through these. I missed what you said at first," he lied.

Cindy went into his office to gather the stack she saw on his desk.

"How do you want them sorted?" she asked.

"Let's put some in a stack for car accidents, another for definite farm accidents, another for any other accidents on or off the farm."

"Makes one a little nervous about living here," she said.

"Why?"

"Look how many people have died of accidents just since I moved here. The odds are pretty high," she said.

"I know what you mean. Since I've been here there was Ed Kurtleman." He put Ed's sheet down. "Then last weekend Amy Sutton and just before her was Louis Boyle."

"I thought you didn't want to put Amy in the farming pile. Hers was a hit-and-run," said Cindy.

"Yeah, you're right."

"Don't forget Clyde Malcolm. Where do you want to put his? He had a heart attack and died when he fell in the irrigation pond. So technically, it happened on a farm, but it could've been medical reasons."

"Put him in the farm stack."

"I'm not quite sure how you're going to draw the line to make your research seem fair. I mean, look at Amy's death. It was a hit-and-run but if the driver thought he hit a deer couldn't that have happened in the city?"

"Hit-and-runs do happen in the city," said Glen.

"I know, but out here they say everyone hits a deer sooner or later so the odds are good. If she were hit in the city, chances are the driver would've stopped or someone would've seen something."

"I know," said Glen. "But whoever hit her the other night had to realize what they had done after the story came out in the paper."

"Before the paper the way this town talks."

"Okay, so our driver has to know he's guilty and now is too afraid to come forward. I hope Tate follows through on *this* investigation, said Glen."

"What do you mean *this* investigation? Do you think he's not doing his job?"

Glen stood up to move around. The wine, the bourbon, his full belly and the relaxed setting made him feel too comfortable with Cindy. He caught himself slipping out more information than he meant to.

"Let's just say Tate and I approach our investigations differently."

"You're saying you don't like the way he works, aren't you?"

"Don't put words into my mouth, Cindy."

"I'm not. I don't like Tate and I got the impression you shared that feeling."

"Why don't you like him?"

"I'm a single woman. He thinks he should add all the single women in this town to his harem and most of them go along with it. I refused. He doesn't care much for me now."

"I thought I was the only one in town he didn't like," said Glen. "You might want to rethink working with me on this if he has it out for you. I can handle him, but I sure wouldn't want him saying or doing anything that could hurt you or jeopardize your job."

"You let me worry about that. I'm a big girl. I can handle Tate."

They continued to sort through papers. Glen went into his office returning with a three ring binder, a paper punch and page labels. Cindy filled out the tabs while he punched the sheets. They arranged them in chronological order within the different subjects.

When they finished, Cindy said, "My, you are thorough, I have to give you that. You should see the stacks of notes and papers the writer's group members have spilling out of their folders."

"I'm a neat freak. What can I say?"

"It's getting late," said Cindy. "I don't want to hit any of those deer lurking around the roads, late at night, just waiting to jump in front of some innocent driver."

Glen helped her gather her things.

"Seriously, do watch out. They're really a problem in this area."

The next morning during breakfast Glen had Angie on his mind. He wondered what she had gotten herself into. If she was just finding homes for hurt and unwanted dogs that was one thing but if she was selling these dogs to research labs or some other unsavory situation, he had to stop her.

He still had time to get over to Ed's to confront her. She came by around seven in the morning to do her chores. He jumped up; leaving his dishes on the table and ran across the pasture to Ed's. He repeated his actions from yesterday morning with time closing in on him. He slipped into the barn and was climbing the ladder to the loft when he heard Angie pulling in.

He settled into position to watch and listen.

"Morning sweetie," she said to the Vizsla.

Clinical Death

"Won't be much longer now. You're looking so good. We're going for a ride on Friday to get you out of here." She opened the cage and turned the dog loose to run around for a while. She played ball with her then went out to fill her water bowl.

The dog barked loudly causing Angie to hurry back inside.

"What're you barking at?"

The dog stood at the base of the ladder looking up.

"Oh no, you're not going up those steps. You stay down on this level. We're not taking any chances of an accident, not this close to Friday."

Angie played with the dog for a little longer then left.

Glen waited for her truck to drive down the road before he climbed down.

"Hey, I thought we were buddies. Can't believe you were gonna give me away like that," he said as he played with the Vizsla through the bars of the cage. "So you're leaving on Friday. I wonder where you're going?"

Glen and Cindy worked every night except for Wednesday researching newspapers. Wednesday night they broke from the routine to attend the writer's group. Glen managed to convince everyone the book project was authentic. He knew he succeeded when a man stopped at the grocery store to tell him about his near-death experience with a combine and a story about his uncle who wasn't so lucky. The combine grabbed him and held him fast. He soon realized everyone had a story.

When Friday arrived, Glen left work early so he could tail Angie to see where she delivered the Vizsla. He knew his shiny black truck stood out as a city vehicle among the farm pickups of his neighbors. He stopped at Avis Rentals and rented a little tan Taurus.

He parked at the edge of town where he had a clear line of sight to Angie's parking spot at the clinic. She had no idea she was being shadowed. With Glen's experience doing surveillance, trailing Angie was a breeze.

He followed her back through town to Denver then onto Interstate-76 to the Sterling, Colorado exit. He continued until she turned into the back parking lot of a vet clinic. He pulled into the parking lot of the store next door. The two lots were separated by an overgrowth of trees and shrubs, making a perfect cover for him.

He stepped out of his car and placed himself deeply into the weeded mess behind a dumpster. The flies made his choice a bit uncomfortable, but he'd been in worse situations.

A female joined Angie in the parking lot.

"Hi, Doc."

With that, Glen knew the attractive woman was a veterinarian.

"How's our patient, Angie?"

Clinical Death

"She's super. It sure helped when your Aunt Eloise let you use some of that money to set up my place."

"This little girl sure does look good. You've done a wonderful job. The incision looks fine. Any trouble getting the stitches out by yourself?"

"It took a little time because she's so squirmy, always anxious to see me, but we managed."

"Nancy should be here soon," said Dr. Bradley.

"Any idea where this dog's going?"

Glen listened closely to make sure he could hear the entire conversation.

"She's going to a little girl. Her old Vizsla, of twelve years, died last month. They put their name on the rescue list at Nancy and Betty's kennel. The timing couldn't have been better."

"Great, glad to hear it. She's really a sweetie. I hated to see her in that cage all alone," said Angie.

"Is everything still working okay with your new place?"

"It's getting better. I liked the other place better, but this works. I'm going to have to find a way to get into the house where I can get some heat going this winter. I'm not sure how to do that since they shut off the power. At least at the Watkins place they kept the electricity going so I could hang heat lamps and use heated hog mats."

"Maybe Aunt Eloise will find a way to help offset your cost for a generator or something."

"I don't know, that could be pretty loud. Did I tell you the new owner of the Watkins place is a cop?"

"One of Tate's deputies?"

"No, a real cop. A detective from Denver."

"Uh, oh. Does that mean we have to move you again?"

"I don't know. We might. He's a pretty cool guy. As a matter of fact, he's the one who took that Corgi, off of our hands."

"Do you think he'll turn us in if he finds out?"

"If he finds out, I promise I won't connect you to this."

"How can you avoid it?"

"I don't know. I'll find a way."

Dr. Bradley looked up when she heard the sound of tires on gravel.

"Looks like Nancy's here," said Angie.

Nancy jumped out of her car. "Gotta go," she said as she ran inside to the bathroom.

Angie and Dr. Bradley loaded the Vizsla into Nancy's car.

Glen took out his notebook that he always kept in his back pocket. He jotted down the license number from the Wisconsin plates.

"Whew. I almost waited too long on that one," laughed Nancy. "Who do we have today?"

Clinical Death

She checked out the large dog running around the back of the Freestyle.

"She's a real sweetie. Take good care of her," said Angie.

Dr. Bradley filled Nancy in on the details then the three of them loaded into their vehicles and, one by one, drove out of the parking lot. It was important to Dr. Bradley they spend as little time as possible handling the exchange.

Glen brushed off his jeans and ran his fingers through his hair, hoping the flies would stay behind as he returned to the rental car.

So, Angie and these two are part of an underground railroad for sick and injured dogs, he thought.

He thought back to the Australian Shepherd. He knew that dog was supposed to be euthanized and Angie saved it from death. He couldn't fault her deeds. He himself had saved little Taffy from the same fate. He assumed Taffy would have been tranquilized, slipped out of the clinic and shipped off to Wisconsin to a rescue facility. Glen closed his book, happy that he fed his curiosity and content his instincts about Angie were correct.

Glen stopped by the library to get in more research hours.

Cindy stepped into the room to speak to him.

"How's it going?"

"No different than any other day. This is not only taking a lot of time, which is no problem, I'm used to hours and hours of research, but I'm not happy with what we're finding."

"Why? What's wrong?"

"There's not enough. The newspapers are too politically correct. I can't get the gruesome details needed for my storyline. I might have to go to the county coroner's office and read the ME's reports."

"Who's the ME?"

"Medical examiner. There might be more details on the condition of the body and cause of death than the shallow story written by the paper."

"You can't blame the paper. People want the facts but they usually don't want the gruesome details, as you put it."

"I know, I know," Glen answered. "I'm not blaming the paper. It's a nice little rag, but I need more."

"Excuse me while I make a phone call. I'll be right back."

Glen worried he may have said something to offend Cindy. She had worked so hard by his side these past few weeks and now he expressed disappointment in their results. He could be hard on himself and push for more, but he needed to remember she wasn't a cop.

When she returned, a huge smile lit up her face.

Clinical Death

"What?" he asked.

"You said you wanted more. I've got more."

"On that little sheet of paper?" he teased.

"This little sheet of paper is going to produce all the blood, guts and gore you want."

"How?"

"Come home with me and I'll show you."

Cindy enjoyed holding a secret from the detective that had him on the edge of his seat. He would never figure out what she had to offer. He sat quietly contemplating what she might have discovered while she drove them to her house.

Glen got out and started to her door.

"Not that way. This way," she said.

He turned to watch Cindy walking across her neighbor's lawn. He followed as she rang the bell.

Moments later, Josie answered, inviting them in.

"Detective Karst, this is Josie Hinsley. Josie, this is Detective Glen Karst."

"It's a pleasure to meet you, Detective Karst," she said.

Josie, with her soft blue eyes and the most beautiful milky white skin Glen had ever seen, caught his attention immediately. She had a gracious smile and a devilish twinkle in her eye. He guessed her age to be around eighty.

She led them into the parlor where hot tea waited on the coffee table with homemade chocolate chip cookies.

Glen surveyed the room bursting with incredible antiques.

"Cream and sugar, Detective Karst?" she asked with a confident voice.

"Plain is just fine for me, thank you. And call me Glen, no need for formalities."

"Nonsense. I will call you by your rightful title. You earned it, Detective."

After she poured the tea she took her place in a high-backed chair directly across from Glen. She studied him as he sipped his tea.

"Cookie?" she asked as she passed the plate to him.

"Thank you."

He suddenly felt as though he were under a magnifying glass. He spent years interviewing people, sitting across the table from some of the worst specimens of humanity one could ever meet. But this kindly, elderly woman made him nervous the way she stared, obviously sizing him up.

"So you're a real detective. For how long?"

"Excuse me?"

"I asked how long have you been a detective?"

"Twenty years, ma'am."

Clinical Death

"Don't call me ma'am, makes me sound old. My name is Josie.

"I've read every crime magazine and mystery novel ever written. Do you believe me?"

"Why should I doubt you?"

"Isn't it your job to doubt me?"

"Do you have a reason for me to doubt you?"

"That's for you to find out. Do you think of yourself as a good detective?"

Cindy sat back, sipping tea and nibbling the cookie. She enjoyed the cat and mouse game her neighbor played with Glen. She went through the same sort of interrogation when she moved in next door.

"Yes, ma'am. I'm a damned good detective."

"Do you always swear in the presence of a lady?"

He shot a look at Cindy, telling her he planned to get even.

"No, not always."

"Then why did you choose to use profanity in the presence of two ladies?"

"I guess, as a cop, it comes naturally."

"Good answer, you didn't back down. I like you."

Glen smiled. There's something about this old lady, she's one tough cookie, he thought to himself.

"Cindy tells me you're researching deaths in Wallace over the past years."

"That's right. We've been checking out the newspapers and..."

"The hell with the newspapers. They only print the soft stuff."

Glen's smile grew broader listening to Josie throw out her own brand of profanity.

"I've been the historian for this town for almost seventy years and my father before me and his father before him. I have a list of every birth and death since the beginning of Wallace. I can tell you about every fire, every hanging. Yes, young man, I have a record of every hanging. Don't look so surprised. Where would you like to begin?"

"Well, my book is about the dangers of farming and the accidents and deaths related to it."

She leaned forward to look Glen straight in the eye. She stared for an extended period of time as if she peered into his very soul.

"You can't fool me. You're not writing a book. The passion's not in your eyes. You're working. When you spoke about being a detective that passion showed through. You, my boy, are an imposter."

Cindy sat up, confused by the comments Josie made. She hoped she hadn't offended Glen or pushed him too far. She was rethinking her decision to bring Glen to meet with Josie.

Clinical Death

"Now, if you want to work with me, we must be honest with each other."

Glen looked at Cindy then back to Josie.

"How do I know I can trust you?"

"I'll take your secret to the grave and, in my case, you may not have to wait too long."

Cindy sat on the edge of her seat wondering what Glen's secret might be. Why had he lied to her and what is he covering up?

Glen turned to her, "She's right. I'm not really writing a book. I'm sorry that I deceived you. I'm researching the recent deaths in Wallace because I don't feel Tate's giving them the time and investigating they need."

Shocked, Cindy replied, "Okay. I'm glad you told me. But what deaths are you talking about?"

"Whatever we discuss here is to stay between us. Can I trust you ladies?"

"Of course," said Cindy. She glanced up at Josie.

"What? I already told him he could trust me."

Glen kept his work to himself. He rarely shared it outside of the department with anyone except Debbie when they were still married and occasionally with Maggi Morgan when he helped her with a book. But, even then, he never used names or places; he kept those details private.

His instincts told him that little Josie might be worth her weight in gold when it comes to gaining information.

Josie clapped her hands with joy.

"Okay, let's get to work. My life's dream has come true, to finally work side-by-side with a real detective."

"I'm glad you're pleased. Now what can you tell me about the deaths for the past thirty years?"

"Do you want all of the deaths or just the hidden murders?"

Chapter 14

The weeks passed quickly as Glen, Cindy and Josie held regular meetings at Josie's house every Tuesday and Thursday. Glen correctly pegged Josie as a walking source of history. Cindy and Glen spent most evenings with Josie trying to keep her on the right track. Her mind wandered off telling them stories of her childhood growing up on the prairie.

Both Glen and Cindy agreed she must have pulled some stories from her parent's childhoods because, although in her eighties, some dates of the events she spoke of didn't seem to fit.

Glen called the clinic to make an appointment for Mieke. He thought her belly showed signs of pregnancy. He wanted to have her checked to be sure.

"Wallace Veterinary Clinic. This is Becky."

"Good morning, Becky, how're you today?"

"Fine," she answered, wondering who the familiar voice was.

"This is Glen Karst. I'd like to bring Mieke in for a check-up."

"Sure, when would you like to come?"

"How about Saturday morning. Is this enough notice?"

"Sure, Saturday morning would be fine. How about nine?"

"Perfect. I'll see you then."

Becky smiled as she hung up the phone.

"Who was that?" asked Stacey. She busied herself with billing and computer work allowing Becky more phone time.

"That was Glen Karst. He made an appointment for Saturday and he was worried he didn't give us enough notice."

Stacey laughed with her. "Today's Monday. Most clients give us ten minutes notice, if any at all. Wish they were all like him."

Janet came up to the front desk.

"Becky, while it's quiet here before we get more clients in, why don't you help Angie with the drug inventory. I need to place an order this afternoon when the rep stops in."

No one liked to do the inventory, Becky included. For some reason Angie always ended up volunteering when no one else stepped forward.

Clinical Death

Becky, armed with a clipboard, went off to the supply room to find Angie. The volume of the radio had been turned up while Angie marked her inventory sheet. She didn't hear Becky come in. Before she made her presence known, she noticed Angie slipping a drug bottle into her scrub top pocket. She tried to see which drug Angie had taken, but so many of the bottles look identical.

Becky quietly backed out of the door. She leaned against the wall, wondering if she should confront Angie or tell one of the vets.

What if Angie had a legitimate reason? Maybe she gathered drugs to stock the drug compartment on one of the vet's trucks. They frequently ran out of supplies for cattle on farm calls.

She didn't want Angie to think she accused her of stealing drugs. She liked Angie. Everyone liked Angie. She'd been at the clinic for almost twenty years. If drugs had been missing before, someone else would have noticed.

Becky opened the door again, but this time, she announced her entry.

"Is the music loud enough?"

Angie turned to look at Becky. She reached over to turn down the volume.

"What'd you say?"

"I said, is the music loud enough for you?"

"Sorry, I like this oldie station. What's up?"

"Dr. Janet told me to help you with the drug inventory. She needs to place an order this afternoon."

"Thanks but I don't need any help."

"That's okay. She asked me to help and there's no one up front. It's pretty quiet today. Now where'd you leave off?"

"I've done this whole section. Why don't you do those shelves over there."

As Becky looked down the list for the name of the drug she would mark the number on hand. She compared them to the last inventory. Everything seemed to check out until she came to the drug, tilmicosin.

Becky searched the bottles turning the labels outward to read them. She looked to see if any had been tipped over or were placed in a different spot.

Angie noticed the perplexed look on her face.

"Something wrong?"

"There's a bottle of tilmicosin missing."

"No, there can't be. We just got some in last week and we never dispense that to customers," said Angie.

"I know. I remember opening the box and putting it on the shelf. I always remember tilmicosin, it's on our *do not dispense* list because of how dangerous it is. I get scared when I have to hold the bottle. I worry I'll drop it, cut myself on the broken glass then get some in my bloodstream. Ooooh," she shuddered at the thought of it.

Clinical Death

"You get over that in time. I remember when I first started in school I was afraid of needles. By the time we'd given so many shots to the animals and I shot myself accidentally so many times, I got over it."

"Yeah, but you don't walk away from a shot of tilmicosin."

"Are you sure it's gone?" asked Angie. She helped Becky look through the bottles.

"I'm going to ask Dr. Janet if she or any of the other vets took some for their truck," said Becky.

"No, that's okay. I'll check with them later. We're almost finished. If we step out into the hall someone will give us something else to do."

"Okay, but don't forget to tell them it's missing," said Becky.

As the days, passed Becky privately asked each vet if he or she had taken the bottle. They each answered no. Now, more than ever, Becky worried about the lethal drug that might be in Angie's possession.

Saturday morning Glen and Mieke arrived at nine sharp. Cal took them into an exam room.

He weighed her and gave her complete physical. He palpated her stomach and checked each nipple to be sure none were inverted.

"She's in perfect shape. How's her appetite?"

"Great."

"How far along is she now?"

"About six weeks, going on seven."

"I expect she's going to start eating less as her belly swells with pups. You might want to switch her to puppy food for more calories with less volume."

"Okay. I can do that. I'll feed her the puppy version of the same brand. What should I be looking for as the time gets closer?"

"Make sure she has a place to go where your other dogs can't bother her. Do we have the exact due date?"

"Yeah, we did a surgical," said Glen.

"Next week separate her from your other dogs. Gestation is sixty-three days. They rarely go more than one day either way. She should start to dig a day or so before labor begins. If you're up to taking her temp it should go down two degrees within twenty-four hours of whelping. Are you planning to take some time off or are you bringing her here for us to whelp out?"

"You don't think she can do it by herself?"

"First time?"

"Yeah."

"I wouldn't risk it, anything can happen. A first-timer might not know enough to get the sack off the puppy and it could smother. Or if there's a puppy stuck in the birth canal and you're not there to bring her in for a c-section you could lose her and all the pups."

"How often does that happen?"

Clinical Death

"Often enough. You see, the uterus is shaped like a "Y". Puppies take turns coming down one side or the other out the bottom of the "Y". Cal used his fingers as an example to show Glen the birthing process.

"Sometimes we get a pup that comes part way down the "Y" then instead of coming out the bottom, it turns and starts up the other side. Then they get themselves good and stuck in the crook of the "Y". All the contractions in the world aren't going to force that pup to straighten out and come back down."

"Well, thanks one hell of a lot for putting that fear into my mind."

"I just wanted you to be prepared."

"I think I'll put in for some time off. Should I take off a week early?"

"No need. If they're born more than five days early they're too premature and their lungs aren't ready. They won't make it so you'd be taking time off for nothing. Wait until about two days before her due date. But remember to take her temp to be sure."

"So I have to stick a thermometer up her butt twice a day but what's a normal temperature?"

"About one hundred and one degrees. Anything below that, start to suspect labor."

"Great, I'm glad I stopped in with her," said Glen.

Cal laughed, slapping him on the back. "You'll do just fine. Most of the time everything goes as intended."

Glen went to the counter to pay. Becky took his check.

"Are you okay?" he asked, when he noticed Becky seemed more quiet than usual.

"I'm okay. I just wondered... er... I had a question...oh, never mind."

"Do you have something you want to talk about? I'm a good listener."

Becky looked up at him then down at the counter while she wrote a receipt.

Angie came in; she punched Glen in the shoulder.

"How's the dog?"

"She's great. Everything's right on schedule. I'm hoping for a nice healthy litter."

"If you catch yourself in a bind and I'm not at work, I'd be happy to sit with her while she has her pups. They usually manage to do that in the middle of the night, ya know."

"Wouldn't surprise me one bit."

Angie looked at Becky, who turned away.

"Did I interrupt something?" asked Angie.

"No. I was just giving Becky here a bad time."

"Well, by all means continue. She's too good. She needs someone to hassle her once in a while."

Glen left the clinic, ran some errands then took Mieke home. He watched the clock, gauging how much longer the clinic might be open. He drove back and waited in the parking lot off to one side.

Angie, Stacey and the two Saturday vets left. Maria and Becky walked out together. Glen waited until Maria got into her car. Becky was about to drive away when Glen honked his horn. He pulled up along side of her.

"How would you like to go to lunch?"

"Gee. I don't know," she said, embarrassed about the invitation.

"Oh, come on. I'll buy us a pizza. I hate to eat alone."

"Okay."

"I'll meet you at Pizza Hut."

Glen followed her down the main street of Wallace, past the other fast food restaurants, to Pizza Hut. He met her at the door, opening it for her as they stepped inside. The only restaurant in town to serve pizza was busy at lunchtime.

They followed the waitress to a table for two near the salad bar.

"Is this okay?" she asked.

"Could we have that booth back there in the corner?" asked Glen. "The further I am away from the buffet the less I'll eat. It'll save you some money and me some inches." He patted his trim rock hard abdomen.

"Yeah, sure. Like you need to worry," said the waitress.

Glen waited until they had their first round of pizza and salad from the buffet line before he moved into detective mode.

"So what's on your mind, darlin?" asked Glen with a knowing smile and a disarming gaze. It always worked with someone who wanted to talk, even some who didn't. "Did something happen at work?"

"How'd you know?" she responded with a surprised look.

"A lucky guess. I'll just listen and won't even offer any advice if you don't want me to. I hate to see a pretty little thing like you look so worried. It'll age you."

She blushed as she smiled.

"I hate to say anything to anyone, especially a detective. I don't want to get anyone in trouble."

"Could this person be doing anything that could harm themselves or others?"

"Yes."

"Then I think you should talk. If you don't want to tell me because I'm a cop, I can understand that. I have a friend at the library who's really nice and understanding. Maybe you'd feel better talking to her."

"I don't know if it's better or worse to talk to a complete stranger."

Clinical Death

"Tell ya what. Let's eat and I'll call Cindy. If she's home, we'll stop by her house. If you like her when you meet her, I'll set the stage. You know, sort of pave the way for you."

"I'd feel stupid."

"Becky, you have to talk to someone. Obviously, whatever it is, it's really bothering you."

"Okay, we can go meet her but what would you use for an excuse?"

"That's easy. She's helping me with research. I've got an excuse to stop by anytime to talk about that. Hell, maybe we'll even drag you into the project. There's lots of old newspapers and notes to dig through. You're a great secretary. You should be good at it."

"I'm not a secretary, I'm a receptionist. There's a difference."

Glen called Cindy to tell her they were stopping by.

"Cindy, Becky. Becky, Cindy."

"Hello, Becky. Won't you come in?"

"I thought we could use an extra set of eyes and hands. Becky might give us some of her spare time."

"What an angel. It's been tough keeping up with this guy with my duties at the library, him working all the time and Josie next door chomping at the bit for us to keep going."

Becky looked confused.

Glen explained, "Josie is the town historian. She's got tons of old stories and ledgers with records of births and deaths. She even has her own diary handed down from her dad with a personal account of many of the deaths in the town."

"Why are you doing the research?"

"A book," Cindy jumped in. "He's writing a book and we're helping him dig up the facts."

"Sounds like fun. Count me in," said Becky enthusiastically.

"Cindy, how about a couple glasses of tea?" asked Glen. He motioned with his eyes for her to leave the room.

She knew Glen preferred bourbon to tea and she now made sure she always had his favorite in the cabinet.

"What do you think? Can I pave the way for you to talk to Cindy or did you change your mind and decide to tell me after all?"

"You're both so nice. I really don't think I should tell you, though, because you're a cop."

"Cindy, this girl has a little problem she needs to discuss with someone and she feels my job makes me a poor choice. Can she talk to you about it?"

"Absolutely."

"Great, I'll slip next door to Josie's," said Glen.

"What can I help you with, dear?"

"I don't know where to begin."

"Just jump in there anywhere and we'll work through it. Is it boyfriend problems?"

"No, nothing like that. It's something that happened at work."

"Where do you work?"

"At the vet clinic."

"Okay, let's talk about the vet clinic. Is it about someone you work with?"

"Yes." Becky played with the ice in her tea. "One day when I was doing inventory for the drugs I saw someone take a bottle and put it in her pocket."

"Do you know what it was?"

"I'm not sure. I mean, I know there was a very dangerous drug missing. I'm not sure if any others were missing. I didn't do the complete inventory."

"What makes this drug dangerous?"

"It'll instantly kill a person if they get any in their body. It does something to the heart."

"So this isn't a drug that one takes to get high or some kind of street drug?"

"No."

"What's it used for?"

"Mostly cattle. It's a type of antibiotic."

"I presume this person wouldn't be using it for that purpose?"

"She doesn't have any cattle, if that's what you mean."

"Maybe this person doesn't know how dangerous this drug is?"

"No, she knows. We were talking about it when I told her it was missing."

"But you didn't see her take that drug specifically?"

"No, but I just stocked the shelf with it before the inventory so I knew how much there was. I couldn't tell what she slipped into her pocket. I was afraid to tell Glen because he'd have to arrest her for stealing drugs or having them in her possession or something, wouldn't he?"

"I'm not sure what he's legally bound to do. Let me think about that for a while. I might visit with him about it in a hypothetical case so we won't get your friend in trouble."

"Thanks," said Becky. "Glen's right. I do feel better."

Cindy called Glen on his cell phone to tell him he could come back.

He said his good-byes to Josie, who hated to watch him leave.

"Did you two get a chance to talk things out?" asked Glen, as he stood behind Becky rubbing her shoulders.

"Yes, I think we had a good talk," said Cindy.

Clinical Death

"I think I should get this girl back to her car so she can have her Saturday afternoon off. I'm sure she doesn't want to spend it with us old folks," said Glen.

"You guys are cool," she said. "You're not old."

Becky stood to leave with Glen. Cindy walked them to the door. Glen studied her face to see if what she had learned was anything he needed to be concerned about. Cindy's face told him yes.

Becky turned to Cindy, "Thanks a lot. I'm glad I got to meet you."

"Come back any time. If you'd like to help us out you're more than welcome."

"I think I'll take you up on that. It really does sound like fun."

"I want to hear you say that after the first four or five hours reading through microfilm at the library," teased Cindy.

Glen took Becky to her car then returned to Cindy's house.

"Well, does the kid have any real problems?" he asked.

"I'm afraid so. I might agree with her. I'm not sure how much to tell you."

"Why?"

"Cause you're a cop."

"Look Cindy. I'm Glen Karst, the person first, then Karst the cop, second. Let me be the judge of how to handle the situation. I'm not a by-the-book character."

"Suppose she saw someone take a lethal drug from the vet clinic, what should she do about it?"

"Was it one of the high school kids who work a few hours as part of a school program?"

"She didn't give me any names, but I don't think so."

"What kind of drug?"

"She said it was an antibiotic for cattle and it could stop your heart almost instantly."

"Yeah, I know the stuff. Why would her friend want that?"

"She's not a hundred percent sure her friend took it. She saw her slip a drug bottle into her pocket while they were doing inventory and later noticed this particular drug was missing. She told me she checked with all the vets and they said they hadn't taken it."

"Let me give this some thought. I don't want to accuse someone without any real evidence or a witness to her taking that specific drug."

Glen did just that, he thought about it for the next few days. He decided to speak to Becky to find out the name of the person she saw take the drug. Before he spoke to one of the vets about it, he wanted to talk to Becky's friend to find out why she pocketed the drug.

Clinical Death

Stacey or one of the three techs would be the most likely suspect.

His first choice would be Angie. He thought it might have something to do with her underground railroad for saving dogs. Maybe she needed a drug to euthanize dogs she wasn't able to save. If that was the case, he'd have to step in and explain she's crossing the line by using lethal drugs.

Another busy day at the clinic came to a close. Seems every animal owner in the county had an emergency today. The vets and techs were eager to leave before someone else called or stopped by.

"See ya Monday," said Angie.

"You don't work this weekend?" asked Stacey.

"Nope. It's my weekend off."

Angie was walking out the door when she heard Stacey, "Oh, damn."

"What?" she asked.

"Larry Swanson called and wanted Phil to bring this wormer with him in the morning when he works cattle. I forgot to give it to him. Should I call Phil back in?"

"No, don't bother. I'll drop it off on my way home. Larry's place isn't too far out of the way," said Angie.

"Would you? That'd be great."

Angie grabbed the two large bottles then darted out the door, avoiding any other distractions.

She planned to go out in Denver that night. With her mind on what to wear and meeting her friends, she forgot to stop as she drove past the turn to Larry's. When she got home she noticed the two bottles on the floor of her pickup.

"Damn. Now I forgot these stupid bottles."

She went inside to get ready for her evening out. She'd drop the bottles off on her way to Denver.

After her shower, dinner and time with her hair and makeup she was ready to go. Now, nearly eight o'clock, she planned to meet her friends at nine. She'd have plenty of time to drop off the bottles as long as she could stop Larry from being so long-winded, bending her ear.

She went to the front door but there was no answer. Then she walked out back to the barn. She heard voices. She knew she was going in the right direction. The voices grew louder. She wondered if she should interrupt the argument. Then there was silence.

She walked around the corner. Inside of one of the stalls she saw two figures in the dark, one leaning over the other. When her eyes adjusted to the light she saw Larry, unconscious, on the ground.

"What's going on?" she said.

The other person looked up at Angie.

"What are you doing here?" she asked.

Clinical Death

The assailant jumped up, attacking Angie with a syringe. She fought back, but was soon wrestled down to the ground. She felt the needle penetrate her thigh and the weight of the attacker holding her down as she began losing consciousness.

Chapter 15

Monday morning in Wallace, Glen drove along the main street on his way in Denver. His early hours allowed him to arrive shortly before the heavy rush hour traffic. His pickup was usually one of the first to disturb the silent slumber of the small town.

The coffee shop filled with farmers after they tended to their livestock and had breakfast. They'd show up for coffee, rolls and the latest gossip. This morning Glen noticed pickups parked outside the coffee shop when normally there were none at this hour. He glanced down at his clock on his dashboard to be sure he hadn't slept in. He craned his neck as he checked out the pickups.

Activity at the vet clinic was a common sight early in the morning. Farmers often went out to feed and found an injured or sick animal. The on-call vet rarely came in after the clinic opened. He or she was usually the one opening the clinic and answering phones before the rest of the staff arrived.

Clinical Death

Glen couldn't help but notice Sheriff Tate's squad car parked in front of the clinic. Glen knew he lived in town and had no pets. He also knew he had the hots for Angie. Poor Angie, she could do so much better than this Romeo, he thought, as he continued through town. As he approached the open highway his instincts told him to turn back. He hesitated, argued with himself then gave in as Jennifer had taught him to do.

"Damn you, sweet Jennifer, do you know how much you haunt me?" he mumbled as he turned his pickup around.

He parked next to Tate's car then went inside. If Tate hassled him he could always buy a bag of dog food, giving him a legitimate excuse for being there.

"I can't believe it," said Janet.

"Me either," said Becky. "I barely knew him but he sure didn't seem like the type. I wonder why he did it?"

Cal and Phil walked in from the back.

"How're you doing this morning, Cal?" asked Janet as she placed her arm over his shoulder.

Glen continued his observation.

"I'm okay, just a little surprised. I had no idea Larry had any problems."

"I heard at the coffee shop this morning he might have been having some financial problems," said Phil.

"Hell, all the farmers cry about financial problems. What else is new?" said Cal.

"Look, Cal, we know Larry was a friend of yours. If you don't feel up to working today we can cover for you," offered Janet.

"You know, I might just take you up on that. I didn't sleep well over the weekend."

Cal noticed Glen standing near the dog food bags. He walked over and patted him on the back without saying a word, as if to gain comfort from physical contact with an old friend.

Glen respected his silence.

Everyone stood around the front desk talking to Tate about the death of yet another of Cal's friends.

"Who died?" asked Glen as he laid a bag of dog food on the counter.

Tate shot a nasty look at Glen.

"Where's Angie?" asked Tate, walking into the back to search for her.

Becky finally answered Glen. "Larry Swanson hung himself some time Friday night or early Saturday morning."

"Swanson?" Glen paused. "Wasn't he the guy with the cattle where I stopped to talk to you?"

Janet answered, "That's right. You met him. I remember you stopped by to talk about your dog."

Tate interrupted, "Angie's not back there, neither's her pickup."

Clinical Death

He looked at Glen. "Hey, you did know Larry, didn't you? Seems to me there's been one hell of a lot of deaths around here since you moved back. You're not one of those damned serial killer cops, are you?"

Glen found no humor in his comment.

"Come to think of it, you were somehow connected with all these deaths."

"Enlighten me, Tate," Glen scowled.

"Ed was your neighbor. You probably met him when you were house hunting. We all know you met Larry. When I talked to Rosemary she told me she met you right here in the clinic. Funny how you took it upon yourself to nosey around the crime scene, accusing me of not doing my job. How is it that you were the one to know about the cut wires?"

"Any first year neophyte cop would have noticed those wires. Oh I'm sorry, you don't know what neophyte means."

"Are you telling me I don't know how to do my job?"

Glen said, "If the shoe fits."

"Why you son of a bitch."

Tate shoved Glen.

That was a big mistake on Tate's part. Glen's training caused him to react to the attack with split second accuracy. He landed a vicious strike on Tate, bringing him to his knees so quickly no one saw it happen.

"Explain Malcolm, asshole. He died before I showed up," Glen pointed out.

Janet stepped in between the two men. Glen tossed his money on the counter and walked out.

On his way to Denver his temper cooled. He wondered how somebody like Tate could get re-elected every year. He had half a notion to quit his job in Denver and run against him for sheriff. He felt confident he could win.

"Why don't you get the hell out of here," said Janet firmly, holding the door open for Tate.

Phil stood by ready to jump to Janet's defense if Tate tried to start something. He gave Janet a chance to handle him herself, knowing how much she hated to have men come to her assistance.

Tate struggled toward the door. He stopped and turned. "You tell Angie to give me a call when she gets in. Tell her I don't appreciate her standing me up yesterday." He stormed out.

"Where *is* Angie?" asked Phil. "She's never late."

"Becky, give her a call on her cell phone and see if she's got car trouble. Maybe one of us can pick her up before it gets busy around here," said Janet.

"No answer," said Becky.

Concern covered their faces.

Clinical Death

The clinic soon filled with clients and the hours ticked away with no word from Angie. The entire day passed without a call.

After work, Becky stopped by the library to visit with Cindy.

"Will Glen be here tonight?"

"I'm not sure, but probably. Why?"

"I need to talk to him. I'm a little scared."

"About what?"

"My friend, the one who took the drug, she didn't show up for work today."

"Maybe she was sick," said Cindy attempting to calm Becky while they waited for Glen.

Cindy called Glen on his cell phone.

"Hi Cindy, what's up?"

"Are you coming by the library tonight?"

"Absolutely, I planned on it, right after I go home and feed my dogs."

"Where are you now?"

"About fifteen minutes away. Why?"

"Can you stop by here first?"

"Is something wrong?"

"I hope not."

Cindy put Becky to work searching the microfilm until Glen arrived. She watched for him through the front windows of the library. When she saw his pickup park across the street she went out to meet him.

Patricia A. Bremmer

"You're upset. What's going on?"

"It's Becky. She's inside. She said her friend who took that lethal drug didn't show up at work today. She's afraid something happened to her."

Glen's mind raced back to the clinic. He ran the employees quickly through his memory.

"Angie," he said.

"What?"

"Angie wasn't at the clinic this morning."

"Who's Angie?"

"She's one of the techs. Where's Becky?"

Glen's heart rate quickened as he ran inside.

"Becky, did Angie ever show up for work today?"

"No. I'm worried."

"She's the one with the bottle of tilmicosin, isn't she?"

Becky glanced at Cindy standing in the doorway behind Glen.

"Yes."

"Do you know where she lives?"

"No, but I can look it up in the phone book."

"Never mind." Glen called Janet for directions.

"I'm going out to check on her," he said.

"Can I go?" Becky pleaded.

Glen looked up at Cindy.

"We'll all go. If anything seems out of the ordinary I'll stay in the truck with Becky," said Cindy.

Clinical Death

The three of them raced out the door. Glen sped down the gravel roads following Janet's directions. He turned into her driveway spraying gravel as he came to a stop, throwing Cindy and Becky forward in their seats.

"You two wait here."

Glen knocked on the door—no answer.

He went around back to look for her pickup in the garage.

"There's no answer and her pickup's not here. Did she work on Saturday?" he asked.

"No, she had Saturday off. She planned to meet some friends in Denver on Friday night."

Glen called in to his department to have Tony run an abandoned vehicle check to see if anyone reported finding Angie's vehicle. He also checked for any accidents in Denver over the weekend where she might have been involved.

The answer to both inquiries: negative.

"Do you know where Stacey and the other girls live?" Glen asked.

"Why? Do you think she's with one of them?"

"No, but maybe one of them spoke to her before she left on Friday."

They went back to the clinic and Becky looked up the information in their files. One by one, Glen drove to their homes to question them about Angie. Normally, he'd give it a few days, assuming she met some guy and went off for a little fun, but everyone at the clinic agreed Angie was far too reliable to pull a stunt like that.

Finally, when he talked to Stacey, she remembered giving Angie two bottles of wormer to deliver to Larry Swanson on Friday. He wanted Phil to bring it out with him on Saturday morning when they planned to work cattle. It was Cal and Phil who found Larry that morning.

Something didn't smell right to Glen. Larry Swanson hanged himself on the same night Angie disappeared. He feared she walked in on something she shouldn't have. Maybe Larry didn't kill himself. Maybe someone did it for him. Maybe Angie saw something.

Glen had no choice but to include Tate in this. He dreaded turning the facts over to him but this was out of his jurisdiction. He'd stick to Tate like glue to be sure he handled it properly. Tate, a prime suspect in his mind, might make a stupid move or flush out the real killer.

"Tate, Glen Karst here. Can you meet me at Larry Swanson's farm?"

"What the hell for?"

"I think I've got some information that might help you."

"I told you before, Karst, keep your nose out of my county."

"Look, I think something happened to Angie and you should look into it. There's something I need to check out at Swanson's and I think you should be part of it. I'm heading over there right now."

"Fine."

Glen and the women waited in his pickup until Tate pulled up in the squad car.

"What're they doing with you?"

"Don't worry about them," said Glen. "You girls stay put."

Glen joined Tate on his walk to the barn where Larry had been found.

"You sure like to use the ladies to help you solve crime. Is that the way you guys do it in Denver? Here it's men's work and we'd like to keep it that way."

Glen refused to respond to such a ridiculous statement.

When the two men reached the scene Tate asked, "So what're we looking for anyway? If Swanson hung himself there shouldn't be much else to look for."

This reinforced Glen's theory that Tate had no idea how to process a crime scene.

"Stacey said Angie was supposed to stop by here Friday after work to deliver some cattle wormer. No one saw her after she left the clinic. I want to know if the bottles ever made it here."

Their eyes scanned the ground for a trace of the bottles.

"Over here," said Tate.

On a shelf, near the door to the barn, they found two white quart bottles of Panacur with a statement tucked between them.

"Now that we know Angie delivered the wormer, what does that tell us? You dragged me all the way out here for this? Some sleuthing, old man."

"Aren't you even the least bit concerned that Angie's missing?" asked Glen.

"Hell no. She's probably shacked up with some loser. If she thinks she's gonna come crawling back to me she has another thing coming. I'm through with her. Maybe you want her. She's not a bad lay."

Glen calmly spun around and grabbed Tate by the throat. His well-placed grip pressed against his windpipe restricting airflow. Glen said nothing; Tate could read his thoughts in his eyes.

Glen looked around for any evidence that could help him piece together Angie's disappearance. Unfortunately, the integrity of the crime scene had been disrupted. There were dozens of footprints all over the soil in the barn. Too many neighbors wanting to help out or just see what happened ruined any evidence that might have been there.

Glen dropped Cindy and Becky off at the library. He went home to feed his dogs and think. As he drove past Ed's, he wondered if Angie had any dogs hidden there that might require care. He pulled into the driveway, looked around then went into the barn to check for dogs. He could tell Angie's pickup had been there but he couldn't tell how long ago.

He noticed her tire tracks didn't stop in front of the barn where she kept the dogs. He followed them across the barnyard to another building. He pulled the heavy doors open. Without electricity he couldn't see inside very well. He grabbed a flashlight from his pickup.

He found Angie's truck parked at the far end of the one hundred foot Quonset building. He shone the light inside and saw Angie's body slumped over in the seat.

Quickly he opened the passenger door. It was obvious to Glen, without feeling her throat for a pulse, she was dead and had been for a number of days.

He called 911 and waited. Unfortunately, Tate was first on the scene.

"Okay, Karst, you have some explaining to do."

"What?"

"You heard me. I want to know how you knew where to find the body. This better be good."

When Tate and his crew finished at the scene and Angie's body had been removed, he took Glen to town in the squad car. Word flew about Angie's death and Glen being brought in for questioning.

"What were you doing at Ed's?"

Glen answered, "Angie had the barn set up as a makeshift kennel. She took care of sick and injured dogs there. I knew what she was doing. When she didn't show up at work and she wasn't at home, I thought maybe she was taking care of the dogs."

"There were no dogs there when I checked," said Tate.

"I know. They were already gone."

"Gone where?"

"Angie would care for them until they were better then she'd find homes for them."

"Can anyone back up your story?"

"I don't need anyone to back up my story. It's a fact."

"Surely someone else had to know, maybe one of the vets. I'm gonna give them a call and ask them to stop by."

"Fine, you do that," said Glen.

Janet, the first to arrive, was furious with Tate for holding Glen for questioning.

"You idiot. What do you think you're doing? Glen's got nothing to do with this. Had it not been for him, poor Angie could've been in that shed for years before you'd find her."

"So you're saying you know nothing of Glen's story about Angie and the sick dogs?"

"No, but if Glen says it's true, it's true."

Next he spoke to Cal.

Clinical Death

"Karst tells me Angie had a little side business going. She was taking care of sick animals at the Kurtleman place. Do you know anything about it?"

"Actually, I do. I found out about Angie and what she was doing a number of years ago. One time when I euthanized a dog I was about to listen for a heart beat when Angie stepped in and took over. Later that night when I was looking for something near where we keep the bodies of the euthanized animals I noticed it was missing.

"I started to keep track of the procedures when we had to put a client's dog down. It was always Angie who assisted. The other vets thought she was so helpful, always taking over at the end and declaring the dog dead.

"One time I noticed the fluid in the syringe didn't seem the right color. I knew Angie filled it, she always did. It didn't take a genius to figure out she was saving these dogs."

"Did you ever confront her with it?"

"No. I figured if she was protecting the animals, which is why we're working in the veterinary field, I wasn't going to stop her. As a matter of fact, I secretly applauded her for her work."

"So she didn't know that you knew?"

"I don't think so. Hell, she had a good thing going. She wasn't hurting anyone and the animals were given another chance at life."

"So Karst's story is true, then?"

"Yep."

Tate went in to talk to Glen.

"I guess your story pans out. Get your ass out of here."

"Funny, I was just leaving anyway," said Glen with a condescending smile.

When Glen stepped out he saw Cal waiting for him.

"You knew, didn't you?"

"About Angie and her dogs? Yeah, I knew. I turned a blind eye."

"Were you helping her?"

"Hell, no. I'd lose my license. I just made sure to look the other way and occasionally intervened to be sure no one else caught her. How'd you find out?"

"Before I moved in she used my place. I found dog manure and other signs that someone kept dogs there. Then one day my dogs heard noise over at Ed's. I went to investigate. I hid in the hayloft on a couple occasions and saw Angie caring for the dogs."

"Do you think this is connected to her death in any way?"

"I don't know, but I'm gonna do a little snooping. Do you know anything about a missing bottle of tilmicosin?"

"You don't suppose she used it on herself, do you?"

"The autopsy will show it," said Glen.

Clinical Death

"I find it hard to believe she'd kill herself but then I didn't think Larry would either. I guess you never really know what goes on in the minds of your family and friends," said Cal.

"Still think there's no chance of a homicide happening in Wallace?" asked Glen.

"I don't know what to believe any more. Keep me posted, huh?"

"Sure."

Glen called work the next morning to request a couple of personal days. He asked Cindy and Becky to look after his dogs, Becky, because she'd be good with the dogs and Cindy because he didn't want Becky alone on his farm with a killer on the loose.

He drove to Sterling to have a talk with Dr. Bradley.

"Can I help you," asked her receptionist.

"I need to speak with one of your vets. I don't know her name, but she..."

"We only have one here and that's Dr. Allison Bradley," the receptionist interrupted.

"I'm sure that's her."

Dr. Bradley stepped to the front desk.

"I'm Dr. Bradley," she said, extending her hand to Glen.

He couldn't help but notice how beautiful she was. He also quickly noticed the tan line from the gold band on her finger.

"I'm Glen Karst. Is there somewhere we can talk in private?"

She led him to her office, the entire time wondering where she heard that name before.

She closed the door.

"Dr. Bradley," he showed her his badge. "I'm Detective Glen Karst. There's been an accident and I was hoping you could shed some light on it."

"Of course, Detective, anything I can do to help."

"I'm not sure if you've heard yet, but Angie Martinez was found dead last night."

She sank down into her chair.

"Oh no, what happened?"

Glen could tell by the look on her face and her body language she knew nothing of the death.

"We're still looking into that. I know that you and Angie were connected with another woman named Nancy. I know the three of you had a sort of rescue operation going for homeless dogs. I'm not here to give you any grief about that. I just want to know if there's anything or anybody connected to this project of yours that would cause any harm to her."

"No, absolutely not. Angie took good care of the dogs. No one ever found out. At least, I don't think anyone knew. How'd you find out? Did Angie tell you? Are you the cop living next door?"

"That would be me. Angie didn't betray your confidence, I found out on my own. Angie didn't even know that I knew. I followed her here once and watched from the parking lot next door while you two passed a dog off to Nancy from Wisconsin."

"How did you know she was from Wisconsin?

"Her plates. So you're positive no owners ever found out or in any way could have harmed Angie?"

"Not as far as I know."

"I'm going to need to speak with Nancy. I want to make sure she didn't give any of the dog's new owners any information they could trace them back to Angie and alert the previous owners, putting her in jeopardy."

"You don't think someone would harm Angie just because she found a good home for their dog?"

"People are strange creatures. Now, can you give me the contact information for Nancy?"

With the necessary information, Glen drove himself to the airport. With a few days personal leave he wanted to do all he could to find whoever might have been involved with Angie's death. He didn't believe it was a suicide any more than he believed Larry's staged suicide.

Dr. Bradley called Nancy and Betty in Wisconsin.

"Angie's dead. I'm not sure what happened. They found her body yesterday. A Detective Karst was just here. He wanted your contact information. I wouldn't be surprised if he calls or shows up there. I just wanted to tell you he knows about the rescue. I'm not sure what he plans to do with the information. He's known for some time and he's not turned us in."

"Okay, thanks for the call," said Betty.

Jean and Nancy were listening in.

"What was that all about?" asked Nancy.

"We might be getting a visit from a Detective..." she looked down at her notes, "A Detective Glen Karst. Something happened to Angie, she's dead; he's investigating. Allison said she doesn't think he's going to cause us any grief but she can't be sure."

"Detective Glen Karst from Denver?" asked Jean.

"Do you know him?"

"No. I've heard Denver has a good bunch of cops. My friend used to live there."

Before supper there was a knock on the door.

Betty went to answer.

"Hello, my name is Detective Glen Karst. I'd like to visit with you if you have time?"

"Sure, come on in. Nancy, can you and Jean come in here?"

Nancy entered the room without Jean.

"I'm not sure where Jean went. I haven't seen her most of the afternoon. She must've had errands to run."

Clinical Death

Glen spent the next hour talking to Betty and Nancy. They couldn't shed much more light on the subject.

"How did you all get together with this project?" Glen asked.

"Well," began Betty, "Dr. Allison went to school with a friend of Angie's. They got to know each other. I'm not sure exactly how they saved the first dog, but they did. Then they saved a second. They almost got caught when they found the dog a home and the previous owner recognized it. They had to do some pretty fast talking to convince her it wasn't her dog. So they decided to relocate them across the country to avoid that ever happening again.

"I used to show dogs and met them at a dog show when I was passing out dog transport cards for Nancy. We got to talking and went out to dinner then became pretty chummy.

"Angie had a vet tech friend who lived near us and together they worked out a plan to find homes near here. Her friend started using us to transport the dogs without telling us the story. After a while we figured it out and started to help out by boarding the dogs here until they were placed.

"Are we in any kind of trouble?" asked Betty.

"You're out of my jurisdiction," smiled Glen. He agreed with Cal. These ladies were doing a good thing so he turned his head to their entire underground operation. He was convinced there was no connection between them and Angie's death.

"Is there anything else we can help you with, Detective?"

"Call me Glen. I'd sure like to look at your kennels. I'm about to have my first litter of German Shepherd puppies and any facility ideas you can give me would be appreciated. I just bought a farm and might want to build a breeding kennel."

Nancy and Betty gave Glen a tour of their set-up.

"Jean's car's not here," Betty told Nancy.

"I wonder where she went?" said Nancy as they approached the pens where Jean kept her Jack Russell Terriers. "Her dogs are gone, too."

"Not all of them, the Berners are still here."

Glen's interest piqued when he heard they had Bernese Mountain Dogs.

"Do you raise Berners? I have a dear friend, a mystery writer, who lost her dogs. I'd like to find her another breeder."

He walked over to the pen to meet the two large, beautiful black and white dogs trimmed with rust. They barked and whined loudly as Glen approached their pen.

"They act like they know you," said Betty. "I've never seen them like this before."

Clinical Death

Glen couldn't believe his eyes. He found Maggi Morgan's two dogs, Bridgette and Bailey.

"Did you say they belonged to a woman named Jean?"

"Yes, why?"

"She stole these dogs from Maggi, my friend. Can I talk with her?"

They went to Jean's trailer behind the kennel. When they went inside, it was obvious to them she had moved out quickly. Drawers were tossed open; the closet was empty. Her dogs were gone. There was no sign of Jean or promise of her return.

Chapter 16

By the time Glen returned home the toxicology report for Angie was back. No alcohol or drugs were found in the initial screening. Glen spoke to the pathologist himself. He requested a test be done for tilmicosin. He had to play his hunch. He hoped Tate would've requested a more thorough screening, but then he didn't know about the missing bottle. At this point, no one knew for sure if it was Angie who had taken it. In this small town, he wanted Angie's memory to remain clean not tainted by gossip involving drugs.

Angie's death hit Glen hard. He really liked her and now he was even more convinced he lived in a community with a killer on the loose.

He called Cindy.

"I'm back. I'm at my office."

"Are you meeting with us at the library tonight?"

"I can't. I have to build fence at home."

"Why the rush to build fence? I thought this was important to you."

Clinical Death

"It is. But you'll never believe what happened in Wisconsin."

"What? You never really told me why you went there in the first place."

Glen did not want to tell anyone, including Cindy, about the underground railroad project for dogs.

"I had some work to do on a case. Anyway, while I was there I found Maggi Morgan's missing dogs."

"What missing dogs?"

"Someday I'll tell you the whole story but her dogs were stolen almost a year ago and I found them in a kennel in Wisconsin. I've made arrangements to have them shipped to me. I need to build a pen to house them until I can find Maggi."

"What do you mean, 'until you can find Maggi'? I thought you two were good friends."

"We are. But she hides when she goes away to write. She won't tell anyone where she is. She turns off her cell phone and stays away from newspapers, television and the Internet. She's unreachable."

"What if there's an emergency?"

"She has no family and she always took her dogs with her. She assumed any emergency, including me getting blown away, could wait until she gets back."

"That seems kind of selfish."

"Not really. Lots of writers lock themselves away. They have to do what they have to do."

"I'll bet she'll be thrilled to get her dogs back."

"You know it."

While Glen was working on his fence, Cal stopped by.

"Building a pen for Mieke and her pups I see," said Cal as he walked into the backyard.

"Hey, what're you doing here? Did you come to help?"

"That wasn't my intention, but I'd be willing to give you a hand."

"Is something wrong?" asked Glen. He thought Cal lacked the normal luster in his voice.

"I'm a little upset about Angie. She was a good kid."

"I know what you mean."

"Why do you think she killed herself?"

Glen stopped pounding t-posts to take a break and talk to Cal.

"How about a beer?"

"Sure."

Glen returned with two cold bottles. They sat on the back step to talk.

"I told you before, I think we're dealing with a homicide."

"Angie or Larry?"

"To be honest with you, both."

Clinical Death

Knowing he could trust Cal, Glen opened up to him. But, as always, the cop inside limited how much he revealed.

"I think there's been a whole string of homicides since I moved here. I'm not sure if any happened before, but I'd be willing to bet they have."

"Why would someone be killing innocent people like Angie or Larry?" asked Cal.

"That's what I'm going to find out."

"Tate will be pissed at you for getting involved."

"The hell with Tate. He's not doing his job. Somebody has to stop this bastard. I'll handle the investigation, then hand it to Tate on a silver platter. If he won't take it, I'll go to the state attorney's office with my findings. I might do that anyway."

"State attorney will prosecute criminal cases?"

"They're fairly selective and mostly handle COCA cases but they'll take others under the right circumstances."

"What the hell is COCA?"

"Colorado Organized Crime Act."

"I'll bet they don't mess around once they get involved do they?"

"Nope."

"Do you think Angie had anything to do with Larry's death?"

"No, do you?" asked Glen, curious as to where Cal was going with his line of questioning.

"I don't know. You've got me thinking about all this homicide stuff and I'm wondering if she was somehow involved and had regrets and killed herself."

"A good theory but it doesn't sound like Angie. Why would she kill Larry? What could her motive possibly be?"

Glen's cell phone rang.

"Cindy, what's up?"

"I think you should come into town. Josie wants to see us."

"What about?"

"I don't know, but she wants all three of us to stop by. She said it was important."

"Okay, I'll pick Becky up on my way in. Give her a call and tell her to expect me."

"Looks like you've got somewhere to go," said Cal. "I'll get outta your hair."

"I'm not sure how important it is, Josie has a tendency to get pretty excited about things."

"Josie? That old bird who writes for the historical society? How are you connected to that nut?"

"She has records of all the deaths in the county for over one hundred years. She's been letting me go through her books. Whenever she finds something, no matter how insignificant, she thinks I should know about it."

Clinical Death

"What's Becky and Cindy have to do with your investigation?"

"They're helping me dig through old newspapers for information."

Glen put his shirt back on then followed Cal out of the driveway.

"Hi, Becky," Glen said as she climbed into his pickup.

"Hi."

Cindy was already at Josie's house when Glen and Becky arrived.

As always, Josie had hot tea and fresh cookies waiting. Glen really wanted a cold beer on this hot day, especially after building fence, but he graciously accepted the tea and cookies.

"Josie has been so kind as to compile a nice journal of deaths for you."

"Nice, hell. Somebody's gotta do the work. You three are always out lollygagging around not getting anything done," scolded Josie.

Glen smiled.

Cindy said, "Josie, we all have other jobs."

"Nonsense, a real detective doesn't sleep until he solves his case, right Detective Karst?"

He gave up trying to get Josie to call him Glen.

"Well, there are some cases that keep us working around the clock."

"I sure think this case should be one of them. This is your community. You should be upholding your duty as a policeman and a detective to protect the people."

"That's true, Josie, but this is Sheriff Tate's jurisdiction."

"Sheriff Tate? That pantywaist. He might be just the one we're looking at for committing these murders."

Glen turned his face to cough. He had to laugh at this tiny specimen of a woman trying to be a tough detective. He thought the world of Josie and her determination at her age. Tate was also a suspect on his list.

"Really? Sheriff Tate?" asked Becky.

"Hold on here, ladies. Let's not go accusing anyone until we have all the facts. I don't want to be responsible for spreading gossip."

"Bite your tongue, Detective Karst. This isn't gossip; this is evidence. Surely you don't think any of us would leak information, allowing it to fall into the wrong hands."

"No, of course not. I should have known better," he tried to calm her down when he saw the flush rising on her white face. He didn't want her to have a coronary right there in front of them.

"Show him what you have," said Cindy.

"Well, since I have nothing at all to do with *my* life I've continued reading through the Journal of Death."

Clinical Death

That's what she called her record of the deaths of the county. Glen loved that term. She hoped someday to write a good book from the facts. That day just never seemed to come along.

"I came across something interesting."

"And what might that be?" asked Glen. He knew she was toying with him, trying to drag it out in a suspenseful way.

"Well, up until about fifteen or so years ago almost all the accidental deaths had witnesses of some type or another. Men working the fields together or with their families and someone would get killed by the machinery or a horse dragging them or something."

"What's your point?" asked Glen.

"Starting about fifteen years ago, more accidents happened without witnesses. Don't you think that's a bit strange?"

"No, not really. With the improvement of equipment, more farmers and ranchers are working alone," explained Glen.

He could tell by the look on her face, he really burst her bubble.

"But you could have something worth looking into. Let me see your most recent names and the stories behind the deaths."

In her Journal of Death she listed the cause of death from the public record then on the same page she began her story from the local gossip.

"Can you see how Tate was very often the first one on the scene. Doesn't that make him look suspicious?" asked Josie.

"He was dating Angie," said Becky, showing her fear.

"Now see, that's what I mean," said Josie. "He probably kilt her sure as I'm sitting here. I never did like that man."

"Oh Glen, do you think that's possible?" asked Becky, almost in tears.

Cindy remained the only calm woman in the bunch. Glen tried to protect Josie's feelings while calming Becky.

"Becky, relax. I'm sure there's an explanation for this. Why don't you sit over here at the table and look through the names and see if anything looks odd to you."

He thought if he gave her a task she'd take her mind off of Tate being a killer. He needed to find a way to squelch the gossip, calm Becky and stop Josie from accusing everyone she didn't like of committing murder.

Cindy and Glen sat with Josie as she explained her theory in greater detail. He could understand if she wanted to see a connection she could make one seem possible. He needed more to go on.

Clinical Death

He glanced over at Becky. She was crying as she read through notes. He knew he had to get her out of there.

"Well, Josie, we've kept you long enough. I have an early day tomorrow and I'm sure these ladies do, too. Thanks again for the refreshments and keep up the good work. I only wish we could hire you at my department," said Glen.

"Okay, you kids run along. I'm gonna keep working tonight. I have nothing better to do."

Glen went to Becky.

"Glen, I noticed something," she said.

"Shhh, tell me later."

He gathered the notes and took Becky by the elbow to coax her out the door quickly.

"Why the rush?" she asked when they got outside.

"I didn't want to give Josie any more ammunition tonight. She's doing a bang up job all by herself."

Cindy chuckled at the thought of Josie the Detective.

"What did you notice?" asked Glen.

"I'm sure it's nothing and I don't want you to think I'm like Josie.

"Let me be the judge.

"I haven't been working at the vet clinic very long, but I met Larry Swanson, Louis Boyle and Ed Kurtleman there."

"I'm sure everyone who has an animal has been in the clinic," Cindy pointed out.

"She's right. That's a common link, but not enough," said Glen. "We need something to connect the deaths and not include everyone else in town."

While they were standing in Josie's yard Tate drove by in his squad car. He slowed nearly to a stop letting them know he saw them.

"Oh, there's Sheriff Tate," said Becky standing behind Glen, frightened.

Glen said good night to Cindy then drove Becky home.

Two days later Glen received a disturbing phone call from Cindy.

While at the library she received a threatening letter. At first she thought it was a school kid prank. But when Becky called her, in tears, telling her about a similar letter she received at the clinic, she decided to call Glen.

"Look, I'm right in the middle of something. Can I call you back?"

"I'm sorry, sure," said Cindy.

Ordinarily, Cindy would call the sheriff but under the circumstances she had to admit she felt a little unnerved by Tate. She already knew he didn't like her. Having trouble focusing at the library, she paced, rubbing her arms with her hands as if cold.

Clinical Death

With nervous anticipation, Becky checked out every client who walked in the door. She half expected each of them to pull out a knife or gun and attack her. She watched the minutes ticking away ever so slowly on the clock waiting for closing time.

Glen's day passed by without a break, allowing him to return Cindy's call. He felt terrible. He had a soft spot for a woman in distress, especially those he cared for.

He called Cindy as he pulled out of the parking lot.

"I'm so sorry. I'm just leaving. I'll stop by the library. You can show me your letter."

Cindy waited on the curb for Glen to pull up. She wanted to talk to him before someone at the library cornered him about a story for his bogus book.

She darted across the street to his pickup when he parked and climbed in.

Without a word she opened the letter, handing it to him.

It looked like something from a bad movie. Someone had taken the time to cut letters and words out of magazines and glue them to the page.

The words said, "StAy aWAy FrOM kArST and StOP SnOOping ArOunD".

Glen laughed, "Oh come on, someone's playing with you. No one does this shit except in Hollywood."

"Let's go find Becky," said Cindy. "I want to see hers."

Glen drove over to Becky's house. He knocked at the door.

Becky looked through the curtains first then he heard a number of locks being unlocked. He assumed most of the houses in this town didn't even have locks that worked and most certainly not a several of them on one door.

"I came to see your letter," said Glen.

"I threw it away," she replied.

"Go get it."

"It's at the clinic."

Glen slipped his arm around her and said, "Come with us. I'll take you there. I really need to see it."

Inside the clinic he fished Becky's letter from the trashcan under the receptionist's desk. It was nearly identical to Cindy's.

"Just like I told Cindy, someone's having a little fun with you. I'll bet it's Josie. This would be her style, to add a little spice to the investigation. You know how she wants to light a fire under all of us. It would be just like her to use this old movie trick to get a little attention. Let's see if she got a letter, too."

The three of them piled into the pickup and drove to Josie's house. They knocked at the door—no answer. They knocked again realizing, although she was one spry chick, she still took a little while to get across the room.

Clinical Death

Cindy opened the door and went in. She thought Josie might be in the bathroom or napping.

"Glen!" she screamed.

He ran in to find Cindy bent over Josie's body on the dining room floor. He checked for a pulse. Blood spotted the antique rug near her head. He could tell by the position of the body she had fallen and hit her head.

Cindy called 911 as Becky ran to the bathroom for towels. Glen knew she was alive but her pulse was weak. He opted not to move her fragile body until the ambulance arrived. The blood loss was not enough to concern him. The dried blood on her forehead told him she fell earlier in the day.

Tate was the first on the scene. Becky backed away from him. She went into Josie's den to wait until he left with Josie and the ambulance crew. Which Glen didn't like one bit, he'd rather have Tate on scene and one of his deputies go with Josie. While Becky hid out she couldn't help but notice the magazine pile spilled onto the floor. She looked into the trashcan and saw bits of cut paper.

Josie kept an immaculate house. She would never have left magazines scattered on the floor. Becky called Glen and Cindy into the room.

Glen immediately saw what caught Becky's attention. He felt conflicted; he wanted to be at the hospital with Josie, but needed to process the crime scene. If Josie said anything on her deathbed, even if she survived, it was gospel—called a "dying declaration", admissible and undisputed in court. Tate wouldn't tell the truth about Josie's statements and he'd threaten other witnesses. Glen knew this to be true, even if Tate wasn't the killer, because it would expose his inadequacy and he would be expelled from his cushy job.

His instincts about the letters coming from Josie's house were correct, but somehow he felt she wasn't the one who sent them. He wanted the place dusted for prints and those envelopes checked for DNA. Knowing the scene would not be processed correctly he collected and wrapped several clippings with a piece of newspaper and slipped them into his pocket.

He took Cindy and Becky back to his place. He wondered who pushed Josie and now he was even more concerned about the safety of these two women. Someone didn't want him to continue this investigation. Whoever it was threatened the women, trying to force Glen to back off in order to protect them.

He poured a glass of bourbon for himself. Cindy took a big gulp from his glass. He offered his glass to Becky. She turned away, making a face at the thought of drinking bourbon. He took a soda out of the fridge for her.

"Why don't you two find something for us to eat while I change clothes."

Once again he wanted to find a way to alleviate their fear. He hung up his blazer and pulled on a t-shirt and worn-out jeans. He joined the ladies in the kitchen. They had trouble finding much in his cabinets. They grabbed a couple of frozen pizzas from the freezer.

As he cleared papers off the table so they would have room to eat he couldn't help but look at the notes Becky had been going through.

"So you knew all these people?" he asked.

"Yeah."

"How well did you know them?"

"Not very well, mostly from the talk in the clinic when they'd leave."

"Were they nice people?"

"I guess so but they all had something to gossip about."

Glen pulled up a chair.

"Sit down. Tell me about the gossip."

"I don't remember anything about Larry. Oh, this Louis guy, you were there when we heard the gossip about him. He left his wife's Schnauzer without food and water and it almost died. Then let's see, oh yeah, you know the story about Ed too. He was always drinking and running over his Taffy."

"What can you tell me about Malcolm?"

"Nothing really, he hated cats and his wife liked them."

"Did he drown them?"

"Yeah, I think so. Why?"

By now Cindy had joined them at the table. She read Josie's journal accounts of the deaths as Glen and Becky discussed them.

Glen turned to Cindy.

"Malcolm drowned, didn't he?"

"Yes."

"Ed was run over and Louis died of exposure with no food and water, right?" asked Glen.

He grabbed the remainder of the notes and started his own research. His eyes scanned quickly. The look on his face told the two women he found something, something significant.

"All of these men died in the same manner as their animals either died or were treated."

"Sutton. What about Amy Sutton?" asked Glen. "I remember the vets talking about her being careless with her dogs and they were being run over and shot at for running at large."

"What about the guy who hung himself?" asked Cindy.

Glen thought for a moment. "The day I stopped by his place, Tate showed up announcing Larry's dog hung himself. He had him tied too close to the fence. Dr. Janet was so mad she left without finishing the cattle.

"It fits," said Cindy.

"That's right. As long as I took the newspaper accounts or the ME reports I missed the details, the gossipy details. That's why Josie became such a threat, she had the stories."

"Most people don't take Josie seriously," said Cindy.

"Our killer isn't most people," said Glen. "Someone wanted to scare you two and stop Josie from giving us any more information."

Glen shuffled through the papers looking for more names and deaths.

"Becky, do you know any of these people?"

"No, they were dead before I started."

"Can you check the files at the clinic tomorrow to see if these people were clients? I want you to read through their files to see if there were any cases that could be construed as animal abuse," said Glen.

"You've got to be kidding. No one would kill someone because they mistreated an animal, would they?" asked Cindy.

"There are a lot of people who prefer animals to humans. I have days when I feel that way, actually most days. I suppose if it was someone who saw a lot of animal abuse and felt it was their duty to put a stop to it. Someone who had all they could take...someone with a big heart, like Angie."

"Why Angie?" asked Cindy. "This couldn't be Angie, she's dead."

The next night when Glen arrived home from work he saw Cindy and Becky waiting in his driveway with their guardian angels, as he called them. He smiled, good boys, he thought. A couple of very capable cops he knew from the task force had been with them since Josie. They owed him, but would've done it anyway because it was brother Karst asking. You get what you give.

"I take it you two ladies found something?"

"Yes, I think you're on the right track, Glen. Becky went back, how many years?" Cindy turned to Becky.

"Twelve years. Most of the people on the list were clients and most brought an animal in that was sick or hurt in a way that could be considered abuse."

"Were they isolated cases?" asked Glen.

"No, I figured once wouldn't count but multiple times would," said Becky.

"Does this mean Tate's off the hook?" asked Cindy.

"For the time being," replied Glen. "I heard he was a transplant, not a local. He hasn't been here long enough to be responsible for all of these deaths."

"My guess is, he wouldn't care about animals anyway," scoffed Cindy.

"You have a point there," said Glen.

"Can we rule out the other vet clinic in town?" asked Cindy.

"I'd say that'd be a good bet since so many of these people are or were clients where Angie worked."

Clinical Death

Glen turned to Becky, "Do you know how long everyone has worked there?"

"I don't know about Maria or Susie, but Angie's worked there for a long time. So has Stacey."

"Then there's the three vets," added Glen.

"I can't believe it would be any of them," said Becky. "Phil's so quiet and gentle. Janet's a fireball; she can get pretty mad sometimes. Then Cal, he's like my granddad. Stacey talks about how mad she gets at the clients dealing with their bills and appointments, but I don't think she'd kill someone. Angie would have been my first choice if I had to pick, especially since I saw her stealing drugs and the missing bottle of tilmicosin."

"Cal hinted to me that Angie might be connected. He thought that might be her reason for suicide. Maybe he knows more than he's willing to tell me. I think I should have a talk with him," said Glen.

"Be careful, Glen. Is it time to call in Tate, now that we don't suspect him?" asked Cindy.

"Absolutely not, give me another day or two to gather more facts. I want this case to be solid so he has no choice but to follow through. In the meantime, why don't you ladies stay here with me?"

Glen wanted to release his buddies from their bodyguard duties.

"We don't have anything with us," said Becky.

"That's okay, help yourself to my t-shirts. I'll sleep on the sofa. You two can have my bed."

"What should we do about tomorrow?" asked Becky. "I can't go to work. I'm afraid."

"You'll be safe. There'll be people in and out of the clinic all day long. Just make sure you don't leave alone or stay late. Glen left the room and returned with two small .38 caliber revolvers and, despite their objections, spent the next two hours teaching them how to use them.

When finished he reminded them, "Whenever you're alone or vulnerable, you *will* have your purse with you and you *will* have the gun in your hand inside your purse. If the bad guy comes, you *will* point your purse at him or her and squeeze the trigger over and over again until they stop being bad."

He made them repeat the exercise fifty times in a number of different scenarios relying on his expertise from his women's self-defense classes. "Vigilance, not paranoia," Glen stressed. "And don't worry, I'll buy you new purses if yours comes up with holes in them. I'll pick you two up after work and bring you here. No one has to know you're staying with me. Your cars will be parked at your houses."

Both Becky and Cindy had a tough day at work. They worried about each other, they worried about Glen and they worried about Josie, who still remained unconscious.

Clinical Death

After work, Glen had the two women safely secured in his house stocked with groceries he picked up in Denver. Buying groceries locally could draw attention to company at his house. He called Cal.

"Cal, Glen. Are you busy?"

"Not at the moment, what do ya need? Is your dog okay?"

"Oh yeah, Mieke's fine. I want to talk to you some more about Angie."

"What about Angie?"

"I'd rather talk in person."

Glen always relied upon his ability to read people when he needed serious answers.

"Phil and I are supposed to go do a c-section on a cow tonight over at Swanson's."

"Who's taking care of his cattle now that he's gone?"

"His brother and him were partners. He still has the cattle there since he lives in town."

"Isn't it a little late to be calving?"

"Yeah, one of his neighbor's bulls got in his herd and bred some of the cows before he got him out."

"Do you want me to meet you there?"

"That'd be great. We can talk after we're finished. Maybe I'll buy you a beer."

Glen explained to the girls his plans to meet Cal and Phil at the Swanson farm.

Patricia A. Bremmer

"I'll be back later. I'm going to leave Mieke in the backyard but I want you girls to keep Cheyenne in here with you and don't answer the door. I'm not expecting any company."

"Can you take Taffy with you?" asked Cindy.

"Sure, why?"

"Her pacing and whining makes me nervous. She seems to bark at every little sound."

"I think she's nervous because you two are nervous. But I'll take her with."

When Glen arrived on the scene, Cal and Phil were nearly finished with the c-section. A large black white-faced heifer lay at their feet, blinking her eyes and shaking her head. Her entrance into the world was a quick one after her mother spent most of the day in labor. The first calf heifer had trouble giving birth and was lucky Larry's brother noticed her standing alone in the trees.

"What brings you here?" asked Phil. "Is that Kurtleman's little dog?"

Glen looked down at Taffy standing next to him.

"Yep, that's her. I came by to talk with Cal."

"Well, if Glen's here to help you, I'm outta here. I've got a family dinner tonight," said Phil.

He took off his jumpsuit and rubber gloves rolling them into a ball and stuffing them in the back of his pickup.

"What can I do to help?" asked Glen.

Clinical Death

"Well, I'm pretty much done here," Cal said as he finished sewing up the cow.

"What's so urgent about Angie? You have some new information?"

"I think I've found a common thread."

"You mean between Larry and Angie's deaths?"

"No, Cal. Between more than a couple dozen deaths over the past twelve to fifteen years."

Cal stopped suturing to look over his glasses into Glen's face. His blue eyes and tanned skin were worn from years of being overworked.

"Glen, I told you before there's been no homicides here in this county for over a hundred years. I'm not completely sure Angie and Larry were anything but suicides."

"I know, but it seems all these deaths in question had no witnesses. All of them were clients from the clinic..."

"My clinic?"

"Yes, and all of them had a history of some sort of animal abuse."

"You don't say?"

Cal finished the stitches with one final knot.

"Say, can you run up to my truck and grab a bottle of antibiotics and a syringe for this girl. Operating out here in the dirt isn't the most sanitary way to handle a c-section."

Patricia A. Bremmer

"Sure, what's it called?"

"It's in a brown bottle and it's called tilmicosin. You'll find it in the top left corner of my drug box."

Glen gave Cal a strange look. Hearing the word tilmicosin sent chills down his spine.

He handed the syringe and bottle to Cal.

"Here, you hold her head just like this and when I give her the shot, slip the rope off and let her go."

Glen took over while Cal stepped behind him to fill the syringe.

Just then Taffy barked, leaping forward, biting Cal in the back of his thigh.

Glen turned quickly to find Cal with his arm raised over his head, about to plant the needle in Glen's neck. Taffy's bite distracted Cal. He reached down to grab his leg. Glen dropped to the ground, rolled out of the way and sprang to his feet.

"You little bitch," Cal yelled, as Taffy attacked him again, drawing blood.

In one quick movement, Glen knocked the syringe from Cal's hand and twisted his arms behind his back. He used the rope he still had in his hand, looping it around Cal's wrists in lieu of his cuffs.

"Why Cal? Why?" Glen said with tears in his eyes. His lifelong love and respect for Cal shattered in seconds.

"I had to stop you. I had to stop them. No one should be allowed to abuse animals. It was my duty as a veterinarian. I had to follow the Golden Rule of my oath as a vet to *relieve the suffering of animals.*"

Now it's time to test "*your*" ability as a detective. Can you find the "Elusive Clue"?

It's a word puzzle hidden within the story.

The answer to the puzzle will spell out the name of the killer.

To solve the puzzle:

A. You must locate the page or pages containing the puzzle.

B. Locate the letters you will need to unscramble the name of the killer.

I hope you enjoyed this book. If you haven't already read them, try "Tryst with Dolphins", the sequel "Dolphins' Echo", "Death Foreshadowed", "Victim Wanted" and "Crystal Widow" for more exciting mysteries and once again the challenge of finding that "elusive clue".

Patricia A. Bremmer